Roman:
The Beginning

Rodney Hall

ISBN: 978-1-951838-17-1

Published by: 90 Day Legacy Builders

Table of Contents

Epilogue

"HERE"

Daydreaming again. I've been doing that lately, HERE. My thoughts have been running wild thinking about what I would do: IF. I mean, would I be kicking it with my family, would I be at church, would I be playing with my children, or would I be making love to my woman? Who knows? Only God knows, but before I was HERE, I was there. There is a place of many turns and journeys in life that I want to share with you, so let me take you there. But not too fast because I have a lot to say, and hopefully, what you read will make you want to read more. Whoever you are and wherever you are, it's time for you and I to gel. Be it man, woman, boy, or girl; if you're in an office, in a bedroom, in your living room, or a prison cell, it's time for you and I to gel. So turn the page and allow me to set the stage there.

CHAPTER I

This is a story about Roman Chance, and most people call him "Man," and I'm about to share some things that happened in Roman's life. I believe in memories and things sticking with you. One memory involved his mother, Faye Chance.

When Roman was younger, he would tell his mom that "When I grow up, I wanna be a player just like my daddy," and she would narrow her eyes and say: "Little boyyyy! I'm about two seconds off your behind! What have I told you about trying to be mannish?" Roman would smile and say something smart, hoping she would let it slide, but this day, he should've kept his mouth shut! In the fourth grade, he was attending Swayze Elementary School in Monroe, Louisiana, when he got caught in the girl's restroom trying to sex two girls. Roman forgot who snitched or busted them, but when the principal called and told his mom, that was a wrap. She tore his butt up! He can still feel the whipping now! But listen, would you have turned those girls down? I didn't think so. There Roman was in the fourth grade, living the fantasy of every male (young or old). A menage, a trois. So in his young mind, he had hit the jackpot with those two girls: Shay and Dream. Here's what happened.

"Roman! I can't believe you!" Faye shouted at Roman in the living room after they made it home with her ranting and raving the whole way. She was livid!

"What have I told you about trying to sex these fast tail girls?!" she continued.

"Mama, they forced me. I didn't want to do it," Roman lied, smirking.

"That was the last straw!" Faye hissed as she grabbed his arm and started pulling him toward her bedroom. Roman yelled and protested the whole way!

"Mama! Wait, Mama! What did I do? They wanted it!" trying to get away from Faye. "I got your 'wanted it'!" Faye said as she went through her dresser drawers, looking for her belt while holding on to him. She tightened her grip because she knew if she let him go, she would have to chase him. She found the belt in the second drawer! Roman's eyes grew wide, his curly hair moving fast as he shook his head, trying to convince Faye not to whip him.

"Mama-" he started but stopped with "owww-" as the first lick came. Faye talked to him as she whipped him. "Lil boy-" whap!-"I'm-"-whap!-"not-"-whap! -"playing-"-whap! -"-with you" as she continued. Roman yelled and cried trying his best to get away to no avail or so it seemed because Roman bent over, came out of his shirt and took off running! Faye was right behind him every step of the way! They ran down the hall, into the living room, through the kitchen, and back down the hall. Faye was getting tired. Roman ran in his room and slammed the door, pressing his arms against the door, trying to keep it closed.

"Open this door!" Faye yelled as she tried to open it. Finally, she leaned her hip into it and Roman stumbled back. Tears streaked down his face as his chest heaved.

"What is wrong with you?!" Faye shouted as she stood in the doorway breathing hard. He just looked at Faye. "Do you hear me?!" she said, tilting her head.

"Yes ma'am," he said through sniffles and tears. She lifted her right hand with the belt in it and pointed at him saying, "You better not come out of this room until I tell you!" She was more tired than angry now. She stood there looking at him crying and sighed deeply.

"Roman, I don't like whipping you. I do it because I love you," she said as he looked at her.

"You-cou- could-'ve foo-led me," he said, hiccupping and sniffling.

"What did you say!" Faye asked, her expression changing.

"Nothing," Roman mumbled, looking at the floor.

She sighed saying, "I'll call you when it's time to eat," as she walked out the door closing it behind her. Roman dove on his bed, laying on his stomach, and rested his head on his arms as he cried and mumbled, "I want my daddy! I want to live with my daddy." He was so busy crying and mumbling to himself that he didn't even hear the door open or his sister come into his room.

"Man," Isha whispered. "Man," she said again.

"What!" he snapped, raising his head to look at her.

"Are you all right?" she asked, sucking her thumb as she sat on his bed, ignoring his tone.

"Why do you always ask stupid questions? Get your thumb out of your mouth! I know it stinks!" he said as he frowned at his sister. She popped her thumb out of her mouth and stood up saying, "I just wanted to make sure you were okay! It's not my fault you got a whipping!" she continued as she walked toward the door.

"Shut up!" Man yelled, looking back at his sister and propping up on his elbows.

"Hmph!" You need to leave those fast tail girls alone! Isha yelled back, working her neck with her hands on her hips.

"Naw! You need to get out of my room! Mamma!" he yelled. Isha got out of his room in a hurry, slamming the door behind her.

"Who is that slamming my doors! Roman!" Faye yelled.

"That was me, Mama. I'm sorry!" Isha replied quickly.

"All right, little girl!" Faye said sternly. Roman smiled and giggled as he heard the exchange.

"Yeah, you better go sit down," he said as he laughed. He exhaled deeply and, resting his head on his arms, he suddenly felt tired and soon was asleep. He didn't even feel it coming. When Faye came to get him, he was still out like a light so she let him sleep. She would let him bathe and eat in the morning.

The next day Roman sat in class looking at the clock on the wall, anxious for the bell to ring for recess. The teacher, Ms. Ice, sat at her desk grading papers. She told the class to remain seated and talk quietly until the bell rang. Roman sat next to a very pretty girl he liked named Leslie. She was a tall, light-skinned girl with long pretty hair and dark eyes. Roman was looking at her, thinking of a master plan.

"Psst! Psst!" he whispered to get her attention. She paused with her pencil in her hand and tilted her head to the side to look at Roman, causing her long hair to fall to the side. Roman smiled when she looked and whispered, "What are you doing at recess?"

She furrowed her brows and shook her head as she whispered, "Nothing. Why?" with a questioning look on her face.

"Cuz I want to talk to you," he whispered.

"About what?" Leslie said slowly, looking suspicious.

"You and me," he whispered, raising his eyebrows. Leslie caught on to what he was saying and shook her head no and whispering, "Uh-Uh, Man! I heard about you: Shay and Dream! That's why they're not here now!" as she looked around to see if anybody was listening.

"Tsk. How do you know that?" he whispered.

"Because I do," she said, smirking.

He looked around to make sure nobody was looking and smiled at her whispering, "Well… just so you know I was gonna show you this as he showed her his penis.

Her eyes bucked as she gasped and said loudly, "Boy, you're crazy!" He quickly put it back in his pants and dropped his hands in his lap to make it look like he wasn't doing anything.

Students started laughing at Leslie and Ms. Ice looked at her asking her, "Leslie, what's the problem?"

Leslie was startled as she looked at Ms. Ice and lied saying, "Uhh- nothing, Ms. Ice. I was having a bad daydream." Some kids laughed. "Quiet!" Ms. Ice said sternly and there was silence.

"You know there's no sleeping in my class, young lady," she told Leslie, looking at her sternly.

Leslie was embarrassed as she dropped her head mumbling, "Yes ma'am." Leslie glanced over at Roman.

He smiled and whispered, "Don't call me *boy*. Call me *Man*," as he winked at her. She was shocked. She just turned her head and didn't look at him again.

Finally! Recess! "Throw the ball, Roman!" Joe yelled as Roman picked it up after it landed near his feet. He threw it back and was trying to find something to do.

Joe called him, "Hey Man, come here."

"What's up?" Man asked as he walked over to him. Mario, Steve, and Foley came too.

"Are you coming to football practice today?" he asked Roman. "Yeah. Why?" Man asked, taking the football and throwing it up in the air.

"Cuz we're gonna meet on the baseball field before we go to practice," he responded. The others looked at each other and nodded in agreement.

"Alright. I got to walk my sister home first."

"Yeah. Well... come and look in my backpack." They walked toward it, and when Joe opened it up, Roman looked inside.

"Say! Where did you get this?" he asked, looking up at him and the others. There was a joint and a small bottle of vodka inside. They laughed.

"My brother gave them to me," Joe answered.

"Where are we gonna do it?" Roman asked as he zipped it up and gave it back.

"On the baseball field," they answered.

"Bet." Roman said.

"My brother and sister said you can drink a lot of vodka and not even smell it," Mario said, drinking some and passing it.

"Your entire family are alcoholics," said Steve and took a drink. "So!" Mario frowned as he snatched the bottle back and took another swig.

"Pass the joint, Roman!" Foley said, ready to hit it. Blowing out smoke, Roman passed it to Foley, then he passed it to Joe, and the order kept going.

"We need to hurry up! We can't be late for practice!" Steve said anxiously. They finally finished and headed to practice. They tried to hide the effects of what they had done earlier, but were laughing as they messed up plays. Their coach watched them and wondered what was so funny. If he only knew. Everything was going fine until Roman got hit and lost the ball. He caught a pass and Steve hit him hard. Steve went low, Man went high, and the ball went flying. Steve recovered the ball and started running the other way. It looked like Steve would get to the end zone until Man caught up with him, grabbed him, and bit him as hard as he could as they both went down.

All you heard was yelling as Steve cried, "Get him off me! Get him off me! Man, stop biting me!"

"Let him go, Chance!" the coach said as his assistants ran and pulled him off Steve.

"What's wrong with you! Why did you bite him?" the coach asked with anger in his voice.

"He took the ball," Man said, breathing hard.

"You fumbled!" the coach said as he looked incredulously at him.

"I know, but I had the ball first!" Roman said angrily.

"What?" the coach said, trying hard not to laugh but couldn't help it. Neither could anyone else, except Steve. He looked at

Roman as he said, "Man, you're stupid!" as he rubbed his neck and walked off the field.

Roman sat thinking. *Well, this is my last year at Swayze. I'm graduating! I will finally be in the seventh grade. I hope me and my friends go to the same school. I don't know though because we moved from the projects on Bonner Drive off Burg Jones Lane. Now we live in a nice neighborhood on Nevada Drive. I can't believe we have a house now! It has a carport, a fenced backyard, a patio, and carpet. We can even walk in this neighborhood at night.* Roman told his cousin Frenchie that his mama's rich! She laughed and called him stupid, but Roman didn't care. They were out of the projects. He didn't have to fight almost every day and nobody tried to break into their place. Roman remembered when his mom would tell him and Isha to watch the clothes she had put on the clothesline so nobody would steal them. Roman's mom also remarried. She married a guy named Frank Black, so Roman has a stepdad now. He's cool, but Roman missed his dad. His dad's name is Paul Chance, and he lived in Los Angeles, California, with his girlfriend Jewel and Roman's little brother and sister: Bryan and Amie. Roman and his sister visited every year. They used to go more when they were younger. On the real, Roman hated that his mom and dad weren't together. It would make his life a lot better if they were together. Living between parents wasn't easy, especially now. There are things Roman wanted to know that he had to find out on his own. Don't get me wrong, Roman liked going to California! The beaches, the parks, plane rides, shopping, restaurants, and family: there's nothing like it. It's just… like I said, Roman wanted his mom and dad together. When he asked them why they're not together, they would change the subject and tell him, "You'll understand when you're older." "Yeah, right!"

CHAPTER II

Well, all of Roman's friends went to Richwood, Jefferson, and other schools because of the school zoning changes and Roman and Isha attended Ouachita Junior High which is around the corner from their new house. Actually, it's behind their house. Roman hated starting over but his dad always told him: "When change comes: adjust."

Roman had been at Ouachita Jr. High a month now and it was all right. It's different from where he came from, but like his dad says: "adjust." There were more girls to choose from, though, like this cutie named Jocelyn. She was hot! Butterscotch skin, long brown hair, cute lips, nice body, and pretty light brown eyes. Roman heard she had a boyfriend, but he didn't care! That day she met Man.

Roman walked into the classroom and sat at the desk in front of Jocelyn. He turned and looked at her, waiting on her to notice. When she did, he said nothing. She looked at him, then got nervous. "Excuse you! Why are you staring at me?" she asked with an attitude to hide her nervousness.

"I'm not," Roman said calmly.

"You are!" she said, still wondering why he was staring.

He smiled and said, "No. I'm not staring. I'm admiring."

She looked puzzled: "What's the difference?" she asked.

Roman moved into her space as he told her, "The difference is... staring is for punks while admiring is for a playa like me who sees what he wants and knows it's just a matter of time before he gets it."

She was surprised. "Oh, really?" she asked with a slight smile.

"No doubt," he replied with confidence.

"And how do you plan on getting *it*?" she asked, stressing *it* as she moved into his space.

"Not how, but when," he stated, smiling. She was struck by his confidence as she stared at him. "Are you a punk?" Roman asked her.

She blinked. "What?" she asked, wondering where that came from. "Why would you ask me that?" she continued frowning.

"Relax." He told her as he chuckled, putting his hand out to calm her. "Don't stare babe, admire."

She laughed and blushed as she asked, "Who are you?" liking him. "Your Man," he said, meaning it.

She was about to say something when a dude walked in disturbing them. "What's up baby?" he asked looking at her then Roman. "Hey," she said while he stared at Roman.

"What's up? Why you staring at me?" Roman asked him with no fear then looked at her wondering if she got it. She started laughing. Yeah! She got it. He thought and smiled.

The guy looked at her and asked, "What's so funny?" wondering what was going on.

She shook her head as she stifled her laugh and said, "Nothing, baby: come sit down," pointing to a desk beside her.

"Nah, take this one" Roman said standing up, "I like the background anyway." he added, meaning the back of the classroom. He walked to the back, found a desk and took the material out that he would need for this class the whole while knowing that the clown was probably still staring at him. Roman looked up and, sure enough, the dude was staring at him. Roman shook his head and smiled thinking to himself, *Don't hate the playa; hate the game, Punk.*

While others were catching buses to go home, Roman was waiting on Isha so they could walk home. He hated waiting for her because she took too long. "Isha! Hurry up!" he said irritated. She stopped in her tracks. "Who are you talking to!" she said, working her neck with her hand on her hip.

"Just come on!" he grumbled, ready to go. They finally made it home and Roman was glad. "What's up, Frank?" he said, speaking to his stepdad, who was sitting on the couch.

"Nothing much. Just working this graveyard shift."

"Hey Frank," Isha said, finally coming in the house.

"Where's mama?" she asked after closing the door.

"In her room getting ready for work," he answered.

"Thanks," she then yelled, "Mama!" as she made her way down the hall. Frank and Roman looked at each other and laughed as they shook their heads. That was classic Isha.

"What Isha?" Faye said as she stood in front of her mirror.

"Mama, can I go over Aunt Jasmine's house this weekend?" she asked.

Faye sighed. "Isha, why do you ask me for something when I'm doing something?" she asked while putting on her earrings.

"It's the only time I have a chance," Isha said, huffing.

Faye stopped and looked at her daughter through the mirror and said, "Who do you think you're talking to, Isha?"

Isha stuttered, "I-Mama, I'm sorry. Can I go?" she whined. "Hmph," Faye said and continued getting ready. After making her wait a while, she told her, "Yeah, Isha you can go, but I have to talk to Jasmine first."

"Thank you, mama!" Isha said, jumping up and walking out the room. "I'm good," she told Roman as they passed in the hall. Roman shook his head as he thought about his sister.

"A straight up con artist," he said laughing.

"Hold on. Roman: telephone," his mom yelled.

He jumped up and picked up his phone. "I got it mama," he said. "Yeah, this is Man," he said after she hung up, trying to sound sexy like that radio deejay on the sensual late night *The Quiet Storm* on KYEA.

Somebody laughed on the other end and then said, "What's up handsome?" and started laughing again. Roman laughed too. It was his dad. "Stop playing, man," Roman said, laughing.

"Naw. You the Man," Paul said.

"Naw. You the man," Roman replied again.

"You're right about it," Paul said, ready to talk to his son. "So what are you doing?" he asked.

"Nothing. Just got home from school," Roman replied.

"So how is it?" Paul asked.

"It's cool. Just a little different," Roman told him.

"Well, it'll get better. Just give it time," Paul said.

"Where's Isha?" Paul asked. He loved his daughter.

"In her room," Roman said laughing.

"What's funny?" his dad asked.

"She just finished conning Mama," he told him.

"Don't say that about your sister," Paul told him.

"It's true and you know it," Roman said, causing his dad to laugh. Their conversation flowed. He and Roman talked for almost an hour and then Paul asked to speak to Isha after telling his son he wanted him and his sister to come see him this summer. Roman loved his dad and sometimes he wondered why he and his mom didn't fight harder for their marriage because it ended kind of foul. Their mom left their dad in California when she was pregnant with him and Isha was a toddler. They've both told Roman and Isha the story, but he blames her and she blames him. Paul was at work one day and Faye needed something from the store. She went to the one on the corner of East 48th and Avalon. She was walking with Isha and got mugged in broad daylight. Faye was hysterical! She called Paul crying!

"Faye! What's wrong!" he asked worriedly. After she told him, he tried to console her and calm her down, but she wasn't trying to hear it.

When he got home, she told him she was going back to Monroe with or without him so he needed to make up his mind because she was leaving! Paul tried everything! He told her it was only a scare and just be careful.

"It won't happen again," he promised.

"It shouldn't have happened this time!" she told him, pissed off. "Paul! My babies could've been hurt! I could've been hurt!" She began to cry as those thoughts set in, but then she began to calm. This was actually the calm before the storm because she told him she wanted a bus ticket for the next day and will start packing! She went into their bedroom and slammed the door! The slamming of that door meant finality! Their dad told them that watching his little girl and pregnant wife leave was one of the hardest things he's ever had to do. He even asked for some time off from work and went back to West Monroe to get their mom to come back to California with him. She wasn't hearing it! To add insult to injury, their mom named their son Roman and not after Paul like she told him she would do. Their marriage deteriorated after that and their dad went back to California defeated and knowing his life had to start over without his wife, son, or daughter with him.

～

"Roman?" he heard somebody call as he was walking to his science class. He turned to see who was calling him. When he saw who it was, he smiled. It was Jocelyn.

"What's up cutie?" he asked as he walked up to her.

She blushed and answered, "Nothing. So that is your name?"

"No," he said seriously. Her smile was replaced with a look of confusion. "My name is…" he said slowly, looking into her eyes, "Your Man."

She smiled and laughed as she looked into his eyes. "I got a man." she said, challenging him.

He looked around then said, "Where? So, what's up cutie?" he asked again.

She held her books to her chest as she said unconvincingly "I was just- speaking to you. Is that right?"

"Well, how do you know my name?" he asked.

"Your sister told me," she said, averting her eyes.

"Okay. What's your phone number?" he asked as he pulled a pen out.

"Roman, I didn't-" she started.

But he cut her off by saying, "Look. We don't have to play games. I know I don't. I'm feeling you and you feeling me. So what's the problem? I don't care about your so-called boyfriend and you don't either because if you did, you wouldn't be trying to find out who I am. So what's your number?" he asked again with pen in hand. "323-4561," she answered without hesitation.

"Can I walk you to your class?" he asked.

"Yes," she said and smiled when he took her books as they walked to their next class together.

~

"Good morning, mama," he said as he went into the kitchen.

"Good morning, Roman." Faye replied smiling.

He frowned. "Mama, why don't you call me *Man*? You know I like to be called that instead."

She chuckled as she said, "Yeah, I know. Other people may call you that, but I'll always call you Roman." He smiled as he sat down on a barstool at the kitchen counter. He and Faye talked every Sunday as he watched her prepare Sunday dinner. He treasured those moments. She asked him about school and if he had made any new friends. He steered the conversation toward something else because he knew she was really asking if he had met any new girls. They began to discuss things in their home.

"Roman, would you help with the greens?" she asked while getting her roast ready.

"Yes ma'am. What do I do?" he asked.

"First, untie the greens, put them in the sink, and run cold water over them to rinse them, then fill the sink with cold water and pull the greens of the stems. When you have that done, drain the water, rinse them again, then put them in that pot for me."

"I can do that," he said and began the task. As he finished, he said "Mama can I ask you a question?"

"Sure," she said while putting the roast in the oven. She gave him her full attention after closing the oven door.

"Why do you show me how to do all this stuff?" he asked while putting the greens into a pot.

"I mean… you showed me how to cook, wash clothes, clean *your house* and other things.

Putting emphasis on *your house* got a laugh out of Faye. She looked at him, exhaled, and said matter-of-factly, "Because I don't want you to ever depend on any woman for those things when you get older." Then continued, "There are some men who can't even boil water. Like your dad," she added, and they both laughed because they knew it was true. His dad couldn't even heat an oven. They laughed and talked about other things as they enjoyed their time together, and later Roman went to his room. "I wonder what Isha's doing?" he thought as he got dressed. He knew she was coming home today because it was Sunday. Just then, he went to his desk and dialed his Aunt Jasmine's number.

"Hello?" Isha answered on the second ring.

"Why you not at church?" he asked just to annoy her and laughed. "What do you want, Man?" she huffed.

"I wanna know why you not at church," he said again.

"Whatever," she said, paying him no attention, then asked "What did Faye cook?"

"Who?!" he said. She knew better.

"Tsk, Mama, Man!" she retorted changing it up.

"That's what I thought you said," he responded, knowing she wouldn't say it again. "She cooked roast, rice and gravy, greens, homemade mac 'n cheese, pig feet, cornbread, and peach crumb cake."

"Hmph! All your favorites," Isha said smartly.

He laughed and said, "Don't hate: congratulate." Click! She hung up on him. Roman laughed as he thought about how he just annoyed his sister.

~

Time came and went and Roman was now a freshman in high school while Isha was a junior and once again the zoning rules changed so Roman and Isha had to attend Carroll High School on Renwick Street instead of Ouachita High School. Jocelyn wasn't happy about that because she and Roman would have to attend different schools. While he would be going to Carroll, she would be going to Wossman and she wanted to be with him. Yeah, he won! She became his girl, and he became her man but it was short lived because of the zone change and after a while, Roman being Roman, adjusted to high school with no problem. He met some people, became interested in the band, and thought about trying out for the drum section. Carroll High Band was one of the best in Louisiana if not the best. But there was another reason he wanted to join the band: "the females" but not the ones who are in the band but the ones who are Carrollettes, Majorettes, and part of the flag corps and that's where his interest was. On a chick named Charlene who was on the flag corp and a junior while he was a freshman. In fact, she was the co-captain. She had been throwing Roman action, and he

15

was feeling her so they hooked up. Charlene was nice. She had skin that looked like dark chocolate, long pretty hair, a banging body, and nice bowlegs. She and Roman had been kicking it for a month and today they ditched school. At her house, they were sitting in her living room talking and really trying to feel each other out to see who would make the first move to something they knew they were about to do.

"Let's go to my room," Charlene told him as she looked at him with that look in her eyes. That look that let him know what was on her mind.

"Cool," he said, not wanting to seem pressed. She took his hand as she led him to her room. Roman looked around her room as she talked and noticed her boots and flag in a corner of her room while her uniform hung on the closet door. Then his eyes landed on her as she sat on her bed in a pair of shorts and a tank top. She looked good. He walked over to her and began to do what came naturally. They kissed, licked, and tugged until they were both undressed with him between her legs, rock hard, and ready for her to get the business. She was looking into his eyes, waiting on him to enter her. He went to reach for his pants and she stopped him.

"What are you doing?" she asked with curiosity as she kissed him. "Grabbing a condom," he said with a smile as he returned her kiss. "No. You don't need it," she told him as she looked in his eyes and grabbed his hand, pulling him toward her as his pants fell back to the floor. She ran her hands down his back to his butt and pulled him closer. He grabbed his hardness and entered her slowly as he kissed her. Her wetness allowed him to slide inside her. They began to get a rhythm and Roman began to make her moan and get a greater feel of her wetness and her warmth. Charlene began to beg him to do it faster and harder and he obliged. Nothing else mattered except this moment. Roman began to please her more and more and she began to let him know with words of: "yeah baby! Right there!

Oh yes! That feels good!" Their rhythm got faster as they both began to feel their end.

"Ahhh-" he said as she began to pant and squeal as she felt herself shuddering. She ran her hands down his back and kissed his face as he lay there rubbing her hair. They laid there until they were ready again and entered into round two and then fell asleep. When they woke up, they went into round three then showered, ate, and got dressed so he could be back on campus in time to catch the bus home from school.

Yeah: he was enjoying high school, especially with Charlene! They ditched school at least once a week after that and spent every weekend they could together.

~

"Man! Answer the phone!" Isha yelled.

"Naw! I'm working out!" He yelled back. He was doing pushups while listening to KYEA.

"Man! I'm in the bathroom! Answer the phone!" she yelled again, getting upset now. Her brother got on her nerves sometimes. "All right! All right!" he yelled, not liking the interruption.

"Hello!" he huffed.

"Man?" the voice said softly.

"Yeah. This is he!" he answered annoyed that the person wouldn't speak up.

"Hey baby," the voice said louder this time causing him to recognize the voice. It was Charlene and sounded like she had been crying!

"Charlene, what's wrong?" he quickly asked her.

She was sniffling as she said, "I-I don't know how to tell you this," she paused then continued, "but I'm pregnant," exhaling loudly. He sat down on his desk and pressed his ear against the phone, saying, "What? I didn't hear you right. This phone must be

17

tripping. You didn't say what I think you said, right?" Hoping she didn't.

She was crying now as she answered, "Yes- I'm pregnant!"

He let out a deep breath and rubbed his hand over his hair until he reached his neck, squeezing it saying, "Aright. Alright. Let me think."

"Think of what?" she asked, crying more.

"Thinking of what we're gonna do," he answered.

"Man, I'm scared." she whispered.

"I gotcha! It's gonna be alright," he told her with confidence, not really knowing what to do.

Charlene said, "Man, I told my mom."

"And... what did she say?" he asked her slowly.

She chuckled and sniffled as she said, "She cried, yelled, and told me she was disappointed in me and...," she paused.

"And...," he coaxed, waiting for her to finish.

"And... she plans on calling your mom," she finished.

"Oh no! Wrong answer!" he blurted, not liking that at all. But then he thought about it and said, "Wait a minute. Listen, let me tell my mom and then I'll have her call your mom so they can talk." "When?" she asked, wondering how that was going to change things.

"Tomorrow. My mom's already at work, so I'll tell her tonight. All right?" He told her.

"All right," she said softly.

"And hey...," he said.

"Yeah?" she asked.

"I gotcha! We're gonna get through this. Now give me a kiss," he told her, trying to make her laugh and relax. She giggled and kissed him over the phone.

He kissed her back and said, "I'll talk to you later and don't forget to tell your mom."

"I won't. Bye," she said.

"Later," he replied, hanging up as his mind started racing. "What am I gonna do?" he said to himself thinking. "Well, mom always told me and Isha that we could talk to her about anything so let's see if this works. He was asleep on the couch when he heard his mom unlocking the front door. The clock on the VCR read 1:33AM. He wasn't looking forward to this, but who would? Faye closed the door and locked it. Roman sat up as she turned around and startled her.

"Roman! You scared me!" she said, putting her hand to her chest. "What are you doing sleeping on the couch?" she asked wondering what was going on.

"Waiting on you," he answered.

"Uh-oh," she said looking at him and motioned for him to move over as she turned on the lamp and put her keys and purse on an end table. She sat down and started taking her earrings off. "Okay. what's wrong?" Faye asked, exhaling lightly. Roman could see that she was tired, but he had to tell her. She was looking at him, waiting.

"Mama, I have a problem. A big problem," he told her, meeting her eyes.

"I gathered that by you waiting up for me," she replied patiently. "Mama. Char-" he started, but Faye cut him off as her eyes grew wide saying, "Uh-Uh! Roman, don't tell me that girl is pregnant!" "She's pregnant, Mama," he said.

Faye shook her head mumbling, "I can't believe this." Faye just looked at her son then said, "Roman, you're just a baby and she is too! What do either of you know about having a baby, much less making one?!" She held up her hand adding quickly, "Don't answer that! Oh, Jesus." Then silence. "So what are you going to do, son?" she asked, looking tired now.

"I don't know. That's why I'm talking to you," he answered quickly. "Hmph," Faye said looking at him and then said, "Well, first of all, we need to talk to her mother." A thought struck her, and she exclaimed, "Her mother does know, doesn't she?"

"Yes ma'am. Char told her and she was going to call you, but I told Char that I would talk to you and then ask you to call her mom. I thought it would be better that way," he answered.

"And why did you think that?" she asked curiously.

"Because… you said that Isha and I could come and talk to you about anything and you would listen, no matter how bad. As you said: 'no secrets,'" Roman answered.

A slight smile crossed her face as she asked, "you remember that?" "Yes ma'am," he said.

"Well, just so you know, I told you and Isha that to build trust between us because if you two need to turn to anybody, I would want it to be me, your dad, or Frank and not the streets," she said. "Oh," he said.

She smiled and told him, "go to bed and I'm tired. We'll handle it tomorrow. Okay?"

"All right, Mama. See you tomorrow. Love you," he told her.

"I love you too," she told him as she put her earrings in her purse and turned the lamp off.

Faye and Charlene's mom talked, and she invited her and Charlene over so they could discuss what to do. Isha wanted to know what was going on, but Faye wasn't having it. She told Frank to take Isha over to her aunt's house when he went to visit his family in West Monroe.

Isha was mad! "Mama, I don't wanna go over there!" Isha said, "Why do I have to go over there?" Isha asked.

Faye narrowed her eyes, put her hands on her hips, and said firmly "Because I said so!" That was a wrap! Isha looked at her mom and shut up quickly! She knew Faye was not trying to hear it. When Charlene and her mother came over, things were tense until Ms. Smith assured Faye that she wasn't there to place blame but to come to a mutual agreement. After talking, they both agreed along with

Charlene that an abortion would be the best answer. Roman disagreed! He didn't think abortions were right, but ultimately the choice was Charlene's and she agreed with her mother and Faye. Charlene wanted him to understand, but a rift formed between them that day.

A few weeks later, Isha came into her brother's room. "Roman, what's going on?" she asked, looking at him and waiting on an answer.

"With what?" he asked nonchalantly, knowing what she was talking about as he lay on his bed.

"Tsk! With you, mom and Charlene!" she demanded.

He looked at his sister and sighed, "close my door and sit down," he told her as he turned over. She closed the door and sat on his bed. "Not on my bed! In the chair!" he told her, frowning.

"Why not?" she asked, wondering what was wrong with him. "Because I'm laying here and I don't like anybody sitting on my bed."

"That's stupid!" Isha told him laughing as she got up and sat in his chair instead.

"Look! Do you want to know or what?" Roman snapped, losing his patience.

Isha frowned when she saw that he was upset and said, "Yeah. I do. What's wrong?" she asked, concerned now.

He told her. "Charlene was pregnant and had an abortion."

Her eyes got big and her mouth formed an O. She was speechless, but not for long. "What!" she exclaimed.

"I said-" he started, but she cut him off saying, "I heard what you said! Why didn't you tell me!" she demanded, getting upset now. "Because, it's done, and I didn't want to talk about it." he told her, shrugging.

"So what happened?" she asked, sitting down again. Roman told her everything and answered her questions. When it was over, she hugged her brother, told him she was sorry, and assured him she wouldn't tell anybody and he knew she wouldn't either.

CHAPTER III

School was out, and Roman was glad! He needed a break! He had been chilling most of the day and took a walk through the neighborhood. He was bored, so he grabbed his keys and headed out. The sun was shining bright, and he had a lot on his mind. He had broken up with Charlene and she couldn't understand why, but to him, it should've been understood. He couldn't handle what had happened. *It was just too much,* he thought as he walked and turned onto Idaho Drive. *And if-* his thoughts were no more as he rounded the corner on Idaho and saw this chick. *Who is that?* he said to himself as he kept walking. She saw him. She was standing in a yard watching a little girl. Her niece or cousin (he hoped) was playing with some toys. She watched him with no expression as he got closer. She was tight! She was about 5'4", petite, light brown skin, full lips, long black hair, Asian-looking eyes, a small nose, and pretty legs. "I might as well shoot my shot" Roman thought as he got closer to the driveway. The little girl looked up at him. *Right on time!,* he thought.

"Hey," Roman said and waved at her.

She giggled. "Hello," she said and waved back.

"Who's your friend?" he asked, pointing his finger at this chick. The little girl followed his finger and turned back around, smiling as she said, "That's not my friend. That's my Aunt Casey" and went back to playing with her toys. She smiled at the little girl and shook her head. She raised her eyebrow when he walked into the driveway. "Is she right? Is your name Casey?" he asked as he got closer. "Why?" she asked with no expression.

"Because I wanna know and I wanna get to know you," he answered, putting himself out there.

"Who are you?" she asked with a frown as she folded her arms across her chest.

He smiled. "My name is Roman, but you can call me *Man*," he said, extending his hand. "Do you always answer a question with a question?" he added. She just looked at him, probably trying to decide whether to accept his hand or send him on his way.

She finally shook his hand and said, "I'm Casey. Nice to meet you." "Same here," he replied. "So where have you been?" he asked her. "What do you mean?" she asked, puzzled.

"Well, I've been living in this neighborhood for a few years and I've never seen you before," he replied.

"That's because you haven't been looking for me," she said smiling.

Now he was looking puzzled as he said, "Huh?"

She laughed then said, "I've seen you around."

"Where?" he asked, not believing her.

She smirked. "Yeah. I've been going to Carroll Jr. High-"

He cut her off! "Hold up! You're in junior high?" he asked her quickly, not liking where this was going.

She laughed and said, "No. I'll be going to Carroll High this year as a freshman."

Roman relaxed and smiled. "Oh. Is that right?" he said.

"Yes. That's right," she said, smiling.

"In that case-" he started but was stopped short as the little girl said, "Aunt Casey. I wanna go in." Casey looked at her, reached down and motioned for her to come here. The little girl dropped her toys and reached for Casey.

She picked her up and told him "Just a minute" as she turned to go inside.

"Wait a minute! I don't know your name!" he said to her back. Casey turned around looking confused as she said, "Yes you do" as the little girl looked on watching them talk.

Shaking his head Roman said, "Not you: her" pointing at the little girl. Casey laughed and the little girl giggled.

"So what's your name?" he asked the little girl.

She looked at him and laid her head on Casey's shoulder as she said, "Nicole" shyly.

"Nice to meet you, Nicole. My name is Roman. Bye," he said.

She giggled and said, "Bye-Bye," waving as Casey turned to take her inside. When Casey came back out they talked, exchanged numbers and promised to call each other.

Casey and Roman had been together for a month and a half now and she really liked him, but was wondering how he felt about her as they sat eating in a restaurant. "Casey? Casey?" Roman said louder, interrupting her thoughts.

"Huh? Did you say something?" Casey asked, being snapped out of her thoughts.

He sat back and studied her with his light brown eyes, caramel bronze skin and black curly hair. She realized he had been talking to her as she played with her food. "Are you okay?" he asked then added "because I've been talking to you and you haven't heard a word I've said, Casey."

She placed her fork on her plate, pushed it away, and then looked at him. "Man-" she hesitated, "how do you feel about me?" she asked, waiting for his answer.

"Is that what you were thinking about?" he asked, wondering why she was thinking so hard.

"Yes," she answered, looking straight into his eyes. He held her gaze, remembering what his dad and uncles taught him. They taught him to never make light of a female's feelings, thoughts or insecurities and to reassure them they matter at any cost and that's why he said, "I care about you, Casey. I'm your man, you're my girl and nothing will change that and if you're wondering what's gonna happen when school starts, don't because we're together." He smiled then said playfully, "You better still be with me," trying to lighten the mood.

She smiled, leaned across the table, and kissed him. "I'll be back," she told him, standing up to go to the restroom. He watched her and then headed outside. When she came back out, she looked around and saw him through the window. She put her sunglasses on as she walked out the door. Roman was sitting on his new Honda Elite that his dad bought him since he didn't send for him and his sister this summer. She got on behind him and kissed him on his cheek as she hugged his waist before heading to his house.

~

"He's a playa!" Stacey yelled as she tried to get through to Casey. "No, he's not! You don't even know him!" Casey yelled back getting pissed off at her sister.

"Tsk! Girl, I do know him! He goes to school with me and Onika went to school with him last year!"

"Unh-huh! Don't put me in that mess and didn't mama tell y'all to stop yelling!" Onika said looking at her sisters.

"Onika," Casey said, walking up to her sister, "I want the truth. Why doesn't she like Roman?" looking into her eyes.

Onika sighed. "It's not that she doesn't like him." she started. "Says who!" Stacey said quickly.

"Shut up Stacey!" they said at the same time.

"Like I was saying…" Onika continued, "it's not that she doesn't like him: she just wants to protect you," she finished, hoping she would understand. She didn't.

"Protect me from what?" Casey asked.

"Well, he does have a reputation," Onika answered.

"What kind of reputation?" She asked calmly.

Onika hesitated, glancing at Stacey who was waiting to see what she would tell Casey and then said, "he is known as a playa and he's been in trouble."

"Tell her what happened his freshman year!" Stacey urged her, ready to put Roman on blast! Onika narrowed her eyes at her as Casey looked at her and Stacey curiously.

"What happened?" she asked Onika, ignoring Stacey.

"I'll tell you what happened!" Stacey said quickly before Onika could answer. "That boy and some upperclassmen left campus and went to that store next to Carroll Jr. High to find somebody to buy them some liquor. They all came back to school buzzed, but Man was drunk! Girlll, he went to class, stood on a table, and started singing 'International Lover.'" Stacey laughed and continued. That teacher was so scared she didn't know what to do! Another teacher came and got him and took him to the principal's office. He expelled Roman and called Ms. Faye. She was so upset she called his Uncle Mark, a Ouachita Parish sheriff, to go pick him up. When he got home, Ms. Faye was trying to talk to him, but he couldn't answer. You know why? Stacey asked with a smirk, ready to give her the answer.

"Stacey." Onika said watching Casey's expression, but she didn't stop.

"Because he ran in the bathroom calling 'Earllllll!' That's why!" Stacey laughed harder looking at Casey not even realizing she was fed up with her riding her man like this and so was Onika!

"That's enough!" Onika said angrily!

"What did I do?" Stacey asked like she didn't know. "I'm not the one who got drunk and called Earl," she added laughing once again. "Well it's over now!" Onika snapped, letting her know that she was fed up. Stacey saw it and calmed down.

27

Onika turned to her and said, "Casey, I like Man. He's cool and he's down."

"Hmph!" Stacey started.

"Shut up, Stacey! I'm tired of your mouth!" Onika snapped, stepping to her sister. Casey laughed! Onika looked at Casey and started laughing too! Only Stacey could make her that angry. Stacey stormed out of the living room pissed, but, even after she slammed her door, she still heard them laughing.

"Punks!" she mumbled.

"Onika," Casey whispered, nudging her shoulder.

"What?" she said groggily.

"Can you pick me up after Carrollette practice today?" she asked. "What time?" she asked with her eyes closed.

"Between 5pm and 5:30pm," she replied sitting on her bed.

"Casey I don't think so because I have to be at work by 5:15pm, so that doesn't leave me enough time," she said turning over and opening her eyes.

"Sorry," she added, "Maybe I can get Stacey and Shawn to come back this way after practice." Casey said to herself.

"Orrr…," Onika croaked, "maybe you could ask Man to pick you up?"

"Yeah huh," she said wondering why she didn't think of that herself.

"Okay, but could you do it in your room," she groaned as she turned over and put her pillow over her head. Casey laughed as she got up and closed the door. She went to the kitchen and leaned on the counter as she dialed his number, hoping he would answer as the phone rang because it was almost 6am and she didn't want to wake his parents.

"Hello," a female answered sleepily.

"Yes, may I speak to Roman please?" she asked nervously.

"Hold on," she whispered.

Casey heard rustling, a door opening, a knock, and a door opening again.

"Man. Man. Telephone." Isha whispered.

"Who is it?" he groaned.

"I don't know! Are you gonna pick up or what?" she hissed, ready to go back to sleep.

"Yeah. Pass me my phone." he asked as he turned over. She picked up his phone and hung her cordless up as she gave it to him.

"Hello," he answered sleepily.

"Hey!" Casey said.

"Casey? What are you doing up so early?" he asked.

"I need a favor." she said sweetly.

"Now?" he groaned.

"No…," she laughed, "but later if you can."

"Casey, I'm ready to go so hurry up," her mom said as she walked into the dining room and turned the alarm off to go out the door. "Can you pick me up from Carrollette practice today between 5pm and 5:30pm?" she asked quickly.

"Where's practice?" he asked.

"In the auditorium," she said.

He rubbed his face and said, "Yeah, I gotcha," as her mom told her to come on.

"I gotta go!" she said quickly.

"I know. Bye," he said.

"Bye," she said, hanging up.

He turned over and went right back to sleep. Roman thought about what route to take as he started his elite. He decided on Milhaven to the service road to Renwick. He wondered what the Carrollettes were wearing today, especially Casey. He laughed when he turned into the parking lot and heard "P.Y.T." blaring from the sound system in the auditorium: "Where did you come from baby and ooo-won't you take me there."

"Yeah right," he said chuckling as he turned his bike off and headed toward the lobby. He pulled his sunglasses off as he stepped inside the auditorium. There were a few people watching the Carrollettes practice as they kicked their legs up high, turned their heads in unison and one by one like a chain reaction. He liked watching Casey dance! He sat in the back row acknowledging a few people. He noticed Stacey frowning at him when she saw him and couldn't understand why she always tripped with him but didn't care either. His dad told him, "Everybody won't like you but just do right by the ones who do" and he thought about that as he smiled at Stacey. She frowned even more when he smiled. Casey still hadn't seen him. She was too engrossed in their routine. When the routine ended the instructor told them to choose a partner, cool down with some stretches and get ready for a meeting with the captain and co-captain (which was Stacey). He looked at his watch. It read 4:45pm, so he got up from his seat to go outside and wait for Casey to finish. As he headed toward the door Casey saw him and gave him a "where are you going" look. "Outside," he mouthed as he tapped his watch, nodding toward the door. She shook her head in understanding, smiling as she went to stretch with her partner. Stacey frowned as she watched the exchange. When he opened the door, he bumped into somebody. He was about to apologize when they recognized each other.

"What's up, Shawn?" he asked Casey's cousin.

"What's up, Man? Who are you up here for?" Shawn asked. "Casey," Roman said cooly, wondering why he wanted to know. "Yeah, I came to pick up Stacey and this chick I'm trying to get at." he told him.

"So what's happening at Neville?" Roman asked, changing the subject.

"Same ole. Same ole man," he replied.

"All right. I'm about to go outside, chill, and wait on Casey. Be cool," Roman replied, nodding his head. As he walked off,

Roman couldn't shake the thought the dude couldn't be trusted. *Time will tell* he thought as he sat on his bike. The girls started coming out of the auditorium in groups with Casey in one. Roman admired her beauty as he looked at her Asian eyes, her light brown skin, those pretty lips, and that special smile that she only had as she laughed and talked with her friends. *In time*, he thought, *in time*. When she saw him, Casey moved her hair out of her face as she walked over to him and kissed him.

She smiled and asked, "You ready?"

"Yeah. Let's go," he told her. She got on as he started his bike. Stacey watched as they left and couldn't understand what Casey saw in him. Sure, he was attractive and a pretty boy, but he was also trouble! She'd seen him get into trouble constantly at school and just didn't feel he was good enough for her sister! He was from the projects and she shivered when she remembered the other reason! "I have to break them up!" she mumbled to herself.

"Stacey!" Shawn called her again, finally getting her attention. "Yeah," she said, realizing he and her friend had been calling her name.

"Let's go!" they said, wondering what she was thinking about.

~

Roman and Isha were eating dinner as Faye got ready for work. She was running late!

She came into the kitchen and asked, "have either of you seen my car keys?" while putting on her earrings. Roman was too busy stuffing his mouth with shrimp jambalaya to answer.

"They're on the counter by the microwave, Mama," Isha told her. "Thank you, baby. Roman," she said as she grabbed her keys.

"I know. I know. Wash the dishes and make sure the kitchen is clean," he said cutting her off then added, "Aren't you late for work? Go to work," he said, pointing toward the front door. She laughed and Isha couldn't help but laugh too. *Silly Roman*, Isha thought as she shook her head.

"See y'all tomorrow," Faye said as she headed toward the door.

"All right. Be careful," they told her.

After Faye left Roman asked Isha, "You gonna block for me tonight?"

She looked at him and shook her head as she answered "Yeah. I gotcha." After eating, he put his dishes in the sink with the others so he could wash them and clean the kitchen. Faye didn't play about her kitchen and house being clean. When he was done, he went to take a shower. When he came out of his room and walked into the living room, Casey and Onika were sitting on the couch talking to Isha.

"What's up?" he said, smiling.

"Hey," they said in unison.

"Where's Nicole?" he asked as he sat in a chair.

"At her daddy's," Onika said she was happy to have a break. They talked, listened to music and then went outside to talk. Casey and Roman leaned against Onika's car as she and Isha talked.

"Let's go back inside" he whispered in her ear.

She nodded. "We're going inside. Y'all coming?" she asked them. "Nah. We'll chill out here," Isha answered first, blocking for her brother. As they went inside she and Onika continued their conversation, but Onika's mind wasn't on their conversation. She was thinking about her sister. She loved Casey and was very protective of her, especially since she had Nicole. She loves her daughter but didn't want Casey to make the same mistake she made in having a kid before she was ready and in her gut she knew what was about to happen. Inside, Roman and Casey were kissing. She darted her tongue into his mouth as he caressed her face and played with her tongue. His hands found her breast and squeezed them, pinching her nipples into hardness. When he ran his hand down her leg and back up under her shorts resting it on her spot, she looked into his eyes and whispered, "I want to, Roman." No other words were needed. He was about to go to his bedroom but changed his mind and led her to his mom's bedroom instead.

"I'll be right back," he said and kissed her lips. He went to the hall closet, came back, and locked the door. He had two towels in his hand and put one on the bed the other on the floor.

"Are you sure?" he asked as he kissed her on her lips.

"Yeah," she answered him in the darkness. He pulled her top over her head and laid it on his mom's sofa, then pulled the drawstring on her linen shorts and eased them down until they fell to her ankles and she stepped out of them. He took off his tank top and sweatpants as she undid her bra and took her panties off. He laid the towel on the bed and asked her to lie on it. She did what he asked, and he explored her body, trailing kisses from her stomach, to her thighs, and up to her breast, feasting on them. Casey began to grind her hips as she experienced the sensation. He found her lips and kissed her as he tried to enter her. She stiffened as she felt him.

"Shh-" he said as she held her mouth open trying to relax. "It's all right," he whispered. The resistance started to fade as he continued and he began to move further inside of her and began to stroke her slowly. She was tight but felt good and what was once painful felt good to her as she found a rhythm and enjoyed more of what they were doing, and Roman was taking his time with her because it was her first time. While he was concentrating on pleasing her, Casey's thoughts were on how good it felt and how she enjoyed what he was doing. As she thought about this, she felt like she couldn't breathe and called, "Roman! Roman!" as it intensified, and she shuddered involuntarily. He smiled as he watched her orgasm. "Ahhh-" she continued until it subsided and she could breathe again. His concern was pleasing her and not himself but before he knew it he was about to get his and pulled out just in time releasing as she looked at him. She rubbed his back, reached for his face and kissed him.

"Thank you," she said looking into his eyes.

"For what?" he asked.

"For making my first time special and being gentle," she told him, kissing him again making him smile.

"I'll be back," he told her. When he came back, he had a hot towel with soap on it.

"Here you go" he said, handing it to her. When she finished he motioned for her to lay it on the big towel. Roman took the towels and put them in the washer. When he came back, Casey was dressed, standing in front of his mom's mirror fixing her hair.

"You all right?" he asked, holding her waist while looking at her through the mirror.

"Yeah" she breathed. Isha and Onika were still talking when they came outside but stopped when they saw them.

"What have y'all been doing?" Onika asked playfully.

"Just talking," Casey lied, ready to go home. Onika knew she was lying but let it go. She would talk to her later. She and Isha resumed their conversation.

"Onika, are you ready?" Casey asked.

Onika looked at Isha and said, "Uhh, yeah. I guess." Isha shrugged her shoulders.

"See you later," he told Casey then asked, "Do you want me to call you?" kissing her forehead.

"Tomorrow" she said and turned toward Isha telling her bye. "Okay. I'll see y'all later and Onika call me," Isha told them as they headed toward the car.

"I will. Bye, Man." Onika said.

"Later," he responded.

"What did you do to that girl?" Isha asked, socking him on his arm. "Nothing," he answered as they went into the house.

CHAPTER IV

"Roman, no!" Isha shouted as she watched in terror as he pointed the gun at her boyfriend Stanley and cocked it. "Roman, please! Please don't do this!" she pleaded crying. He wasn't hearing her though!

"This punk don't know who he messin' wit! You don't put your hands on my sister, fool!" Roman said, full of anger. Stanley held his hands out and begged him not to shoot him!

"I'm sorry, Man! Don't shoot me!" he pleaded, hoping he would put the gun down.

Isha slowly walked toward her brother, "Roman, please. Let him go and put the gun down." she said softly, trying to reason with him. He frowned. "You want this fool?" he asked, his eyes never leaving him.

"No, but I don't want you to go to jail, either!" she replied with tears in her eyes. "Let him go man! He's not worth it!" she continued.

He weighed her words, then said, "Clown! If I see you near her or hear about you trying to put your hands on her ain't gonna be no talking and I know you understand what I mean!" Stanley shook his head in agreement. "Get out of our yard!" he said, getting angry. Stanley ran and jumped in his car! Tires screeching from him getting out of there. "Coward!" Roman said as he thought about when he heard that clown hit Isha! He lost it! He was like LAPD with his sister! Protect and serve! Don't nobody put their hands on her! He thought as he looked at her again, "Let's go in the house." he told her. *Hopefully nobody called the cops*, he thought as he looked around. Only a few people saw it.

"I heard about what happened," Casey told Roman as they talked on the phone.

"What happened?" he asked, acting like he didn't know what she was talking about.

"Don't play Roman! You know what I'm talking about!" she told him, getting mad.

"No, I don't. Why don't you tell me?" he said calmly.

"Yesterday Roman! You, Isha, and Stanley! That's what I'm talking about!" she said, frustrated.

He breathed deeply and said, "What about it?"

"What about it!" she repeated, not believing his attitude!

"I'm glad you weren't hurt!" she added.

"Me too," he said jokingly.

"It's not funny, Man!" she said pissed!

"I know! Look Casey! I'm all right! Isha's all right and that chump is all right, so leave it alone! All right! All right?!" he told her, returning her anger.

"All right." she whispered, not liking this at all, "I just don't want anything to happen to you," she told him with emotion in her voice.

He sighed and told her, "That's over with, Casey. That episode is cancelled. So what are your plans for today?" he asked to change the subject.

"Nothing," she replied.

"Let's go to the mall," he suggested, wanting to get out of the house and spend some time with her.

"Okay," she said, thinking the same thing.

"All right. I'll pick you up in two hours. Two hours, Casey. You know how long you take to get ready," he stressed.

She laughed. "Shut up! Just be on time!" she said, knowing that he was telling the truth.

"Two hours!" he said again.

"I heard you!" she replied, laughing.

"Two hours!" he repeated.

"Okay. Bye," she said, hearing him laugh as they hung up.

When they walked into the entrance of the mall, the aromas from Chelsea's, Sbarro's, and the other restaurants in the food court hit them and made his stomach growl.

"Mmm-" he inhaled deeply and said, "that smells good."

"You're just greedy." Casey said, teasing him while he held her hand. They both laughed. She was looking beautiful in a white Gucci sundress while he had on a white Gucci short set, sandals, Gucci shades and a Gucci watch. They looked good together.

"Do you want to eat now?" he asked. She looked up at him and said incredulously. "Roman, I know that you're not hungry. We just got here."

"Naw. I just know how greedy you are," he lied.

"Yeah right!" she said, laughing and bumping him with her hip. "Come on," she told him ready to go into some stores. They went to Dillard's, Foot Locker, JCPenny, and some other stores. They got some clothes, tennis shoes, socks, cologne, perfume, and some other small items. They didn't want to get too much because they were on his Honda Elite motorbike. When they were finished, both of them were starving.

"So where do you want to eat?" she asked with him grinning.

"What about Sbarro's?" he suggested.

"Uh-Uh. I don't want to sit in the food court," she said, shaking her head.

"El Chico?" he asked.

"That'll work," she said, nodding in agreement.

"Roman, why did you buy those different bottles of cologne when you could've just gotten a variety box from Dillard's? It has five to six different colognes in it and you would come out cheaper." "Hmph. I never thought about that, but now I know," he answered as they reached the entrance of El Chico and waited to be seated. After they were seated, they talked for a while and then ordered. Roman ordered the beef fajitas while Casey ordered the Santa Fe chicken salad. Their meals came in no time and they both dug in. The service was great, and they were both full. After paying the bill, they got ready to go.

When they got close to his house, he leaned back asking, "Are you going home?"

"Yeah," she said in his ear. He shook his head and bypassed his house. He pulled into her driveway and she got off and got her bags. "Call me later," she said, kissing him.

"I gotcha. Later." he replied.

"Bye." she told him, smiling.

When he was about to leave, Onika came out and said, "Roman, wait!" He hit his brakes.

"What's up?" he asked, looking perplexed. Casey was wondering what was going on too after seeing the expression on her sister's face. Onika walked towards them.

"Your mom called looking for you and she sounded pissed!" Onika told him. Casey and Roman looked at each other.

"I think it's about that episode with Stanley," she added.

He frowned. "But how did-" he began and stopped when he saw Stacey looking out the door smiling. "Never mind. It's cool," he said, shaking his head. He couldn't understand why this chick hated him so much. Casey and Onika saw their sister too and frowned. "Call me baby," Casey told him.

"Tell Isha to call me too," Onika added.

"All right. Later," he said and rode off as they turned their attention toward Stacey. As his bike rounded the corner, Casey turned around and frowned as she saw her sister still standing in the door smiling. "What's so funny, Stacey?" she asked, pissed.

38

"Move!" she said, brushing past her with her bags.

"What's wrong with you?" Stacey said, stepping back. Onika closed the door as she came in behind them. Casey sat her bags on the kitchen counter and spun around.

"You know what's wrong!" she told her sister.

Casey narrowed her eyes. "I have a question for you, Stacey!" she said, cocking her head to the side and folding her arms across her chest and asked, "How did Man's mom find out about what happened?"

"How should I know?" Stacey said, frowning.

"Oh, you know!" Onika said.

"Why would you do that Stacey?" she asked, waiting for her answer.

"I didn't," she responded unconvincingly, then smirked and said, "all right. It just slipped out," laughing.

"I got your slipped out!" Casey said charging toward her, but Onika grabbed her before she could reach her!

"Casey, chill!" Onika told her as she tightened her grip around her. Stacey looked at her sister angrily and said, "I can't believe you tripping over that chump!"

"I got your chump!" Casey said, trying her best to get away from Onika!

For Onika to be so small, she was strong, Casey thought as she yelled, "Let me go!"

"Stacey, just go!" Onika said, not liking this situation!

"Now!" she said through gritted teeth!

"For what? I'm not the one you're holding!" she said pissed.

"Oh, okay! You want me to let her go?!" Onika said, waiting for her answer!

Stacey looked and thought about it,"nah!" she said and went to her room!

"You cool?" Onika asked Casey after their sister closed her door. "No!" she snapped, still mad! She tightened her grip and asked again, "Are you cool?"

Casey began to relax then said, "Yeah. Yeah, I'm cool," and exhaled in frustration. She let her go slowly and sat down. Casey sat down beside her.

Onika looked at her sister and told her, "Casey, you can't let her get to you."

Casey said something, but Onika held her hand up to stop her and said, "She's just being Stacey, and I don't know why she doesn't like Man or want him with you, but I do know that she loves you."

Casey sighed, and she dropped her head in her hands. "I'm tired of this Onika! I don't interfere with her relationship!" she said, frustrated.

"Ride it out," Onika said plainly.

Casey looked up at her sister and laughed. "You ride it out!" she told her, realizing what she was saying.

Onika smiled and told her, "We'll ride it out together." Sisters forever! No matter what! That was their pact!

Roman sat his bags on the trunk of his mom's car and went in the backyard to park his Elite. He locked the gate, got his bags, and unlocked the front door.

When he closed the door, "Isha, is that Roman?" his mom yelled. Isha peeped in the living room and answered, "yes, ma'am." She shook her head, and he nodded in understanding. She went into her room and closed the door.

"Roman! I wanna talk to you! Now!" Faye yelled.

"Yes ma'am. Here I come," he answered, sighing as he put his bags and keys in his room. When he went to his mother's room, she was on her sofa watching soaps she had recorded while she slept. She looked at him with anger as she turned the TV off and said, "I know! You did not! Have my gun!" He just looked at her and said nothing. "Did you!" she yelled. She was mad!

"Mama-" he started but Faye cut him off saying, "Boyy! Are you crazy? You could've hurt that boy! And what about your sister?!" "But-"

"But nothing!" she shouted, cutting him off again.

"He put his hands on Isha!" Roman said, trying to justify what he did.

"What did you say?!" Faye asked, standing up, narrowing her eyes. Roman stayed quiet. Faye shook her head then said, "You need to be glad nobody called the cops. Do you wanna go to juvenile, Roman? Do you know what they do to young boys in that place?" she asked, then answered for him. "They beat and rape them Roman! That's what they do!"

"Hmph," Roman said as he frowned, shaking his head thinking, *not me*!

Faye read it and said, "Oh! I know what you're thinking! Not me! I'm bad! Ain't nobody gonna do that to me!" She shook her head and continued, "You're headed down the wrong road, son!" trying to regain her composure. She looked at him, took a deep breath, and said, "Oh… and just so you know, you're grounded until I say otherwise! No TV! No stereo and no Elite!" He knew that was coming. "In fact, give me the keys!" she demanded, holding her hand out.

"They're in my room," he told her, nodding toward the hall.

"Go get them!" Faye ordered, pointing down the hall! He went to his room and got them, taking his house keys off as he walked back to his mom's room.

"Here they are," he said, holding them out to her.

"Uh-uh, Faye said, shaking her head, "I want to see the rest of them," as she took the keys and held her hands out for the others. He placed the others in her hand so she could see them. "Here," she said, giving the others back when she saw they were his house keys, then said, "Just so we're clear! You are grounded! No company! No going anywhere and no Casey coming over here, period! Try me and you will be on the first plane smoking going to Los Angeles to live with your dad! Permanently! Is that clear?" she asked, looking at him.

"Yeah," he said, mad.

"What did you say?" Faye asked, stepping toward him.

"Yes, ma'am" answered.

"That's what I thought you said. We're done!" she said and turned her soaps back on as she sat down. She glanced at her son as he walked out and her anger was replaced with sadness. She didn't like talking to him that way, but she didn't know what else to do! She was afraid for him and didn't like the path he was on.

He went in his room, closed his door, and didn't bother putting his stuff up. He was just tired. Mentally tired. He put his headphones on and turned on his stereo, forgetting his mom told him no stereo. When it came on, the sounds of GQ's song "I Do Love You" filled his headphones. He laid on his bed and thought about his mom and being grounded. He would've done the same thing for her if anybody put their hands on her and, in his adolescent mind, he thought he was right, never seeing her point. He bobbed his head as the song caught his attention: "My, my baby- Heyyy yeah." He loved this old school! His uncles and aunts turned him on to it. He also liked older singers like Sam Cooke, Otis Redding, and Jackie Wilson. This made him think about his dad.

"Roman!" Isha called him again, nudging his arm. He opened his eyes and moved his headphones.

"What's up?" he said.

"What did she say?" Isha asked, looking sad.

"You didn't hear?" he asked, surprised.

"No. I was doing what you're doing," she answered as she sat at his desk.

"Huh?" he said, looking confused.

"I had my headphones on listening to music," she clarified.

"Oh," he said, understanding.

"I didn't want to hear mom fussing at you," she told him.

"Well...," he said as he folded his hands behind his head, "she took my Elite," Isha grimaced, "I'm grounded until she says I'm not so I can't go anywhere. No company, especially Casey! No TV or stereo!" Isha looked at his headphones around his neck and smiled. "And if I try her, I will be on the first plane smoking to Los Angeles to live with our dad permanently! That was it!" he added and closed his eyes, thinking.

"I'm sorry, man." Isha whispered.

He opened his eyes and looked at her when he heard her sadness and said, "Uh-uh! You better not trip! I did that, and I'd do it again! Don't nobody put their hands on you, especially a hard head!"

"That episode is cancelled so let that go!"

"Well, are you gonna call Casey?" she asked, feeling better. He looked at her and it hit him! He smiled! "What?" Isha said, confused by the look he gave her.

"I can still use the phone!" he said, still smiling.

"Okay. Don't forget to call her," Isha said, standing up and opening his door.

"Hold up," he blurted.

"What?" she asked.

"Onika wants you to call her too," he said.

"Okay. In fact I'll go do that right now" she told him and closed his door behind her. He put his headphones back on and smiled as music filled his ears.

~

"Twenty-eight, twenty-nine, thirty!" Roman grunted as he finished his fifth set of pushups and squats. He got up, stretching his arms and did some waist bends to get ready to jump rope. He was

43

stressed and missed Casey! But his mind was on other things too. He wasn't happy and didn't know why. Something was missing and he was in turmoil. He shook the thoughts off and took a sip of water as he looked at his reflection in the patio window. He put the water down, grabbed his jump rope, and started jumping. He liked to relieve stress this way but thought about another way that he liked better and smiled. He was missing Casey. He hadn't seen her in weeks. He had been jumping rope for 20 minutes when the cordless phone rang. He looked at it as he kept jumping. *Why bring it outside if I'm not going to answer it* he thought as he put the rope down and picked the phone up. "Hello," he said, slowing his breathing as sweat dripped off his nose.

"May I speak to Roman?" a female asked.

"Speaking," he answered, catching his breath.

"How are you?" she asked.

"I'm good. Who am I speaking with?" he asked while taking a sip of water.

"Somebody who wants to get to know you," she said teasingly. "Does this someone have a name?" he asked, tiring of the back and forth.

"Yes. My name is Terri," she answered.

"Okay Terri, what can I do for you?" he asked.

"Well, I was hoping we could get together and-."

"Why?" he asked, cutting her off.

"Why what?" she asked, confused.

"Listen. I don't know you and I'm involved with someone right now and we're good so I'm good. You feel me?" he added. Silence. "Hello?" he said, wondering if she had hung up.

"I'm here," she said softly and continued, "it was nice talking to you."

"Goodbye," he said.

"Bye," she said, hanging up. Man hung up and went back to working out, hoping he hadn't cooled down too much. On the other end, Stacey was furious as she looked at Karen who told Roman her name was Terri. "That chump knew it was a setup!" she fumed as she slammed the phone down and turned off the recorder.

"I doubt it, Stacey," Karen said as she thought about the conversation.

"Why!" Stacey snapped, still angry.

"Well, for starters he doesn't know me or my voice and I go to Wossman and not Carroll," she replied.

"Maybe he *does* care about Casey." she added.

"Tsk! Yeah, right! No, he doesn't!" Stacey replied, not trying to hear it. Karen didn't argue with her but wondered why Stacey didn't want him with her sister. She frowned as a thought came to her, *Did Stacey want Roman? Hmm… you never know,* she mumbled as she watched Stacey.

Roman stood in the bathroom brushing his teeth, deciding it was time for a haircut after looking at himself in the mirror. Faye was still grounding him, but as he gargled, he thought, *something gotta give!* He was going to the barbershop one way or another. He wiped his mouth and walked out of the bathroom.

He heard Faye talking as he walked into the living room: "I know. Uh-Huh. You're right. I was thinking the same thing," she said to somebody on the phone. He sat on the barstool at the counter and watched silently as she washed dishes. She turned to put something in the cabinet and was startled when she saw him. "Boy, haven't I told you to stop doing that! Let someone know you're in the room!" she hissed covering the phone with her hand.

"My bad," he told her laughing.

"Uh-huh," she said pursing her lips and rolling her eyes.

"I'm back," she said, turning her attention back to her conversation and the dishes. "Huh? Your grandson. Yeah," she said, "your grandmother said hi," she told him, balancing the phone under her chin.

"Hey grandma!" he said loud enough so she would hear him. He glanced at the clock in the kitchen and saw that it was 8:30am. *Shoot! I need to be there before 10 o'clock because Stamper's barber shop is always crowded on Saturday, he* thought, hoping she was about to get off the phone. After a few more minutes, Faye told him, "hang the phone up for her and wipe it off," because she saw suds on it. "Yes ma'am. Mama, I need a haircut," he told her after hanging the phone up.

"And?" Faye answered, knowing where this was going.

"I need to go to the barbershop, Mama," he replied, hoping she would let him go. He was tired of being grounded. "Can I go, Mama?" he asked, hoping she'd say yes.

"How?" Faye asked, smirking, already knowing the answer.

"On my bike. Mama, I've been grounded for a while," he said, then asked, "can I have my keys?" She kept washing dishes.

"Mama, he started, wondering if she was listening to him.

She was: "Yeah, Roman, you can go. Go get my purse," she said. "Okay!" he said and got up before she changed her mind.

"Am I off punishment?" he asked when he came back, hoping she would say yeah.

She chuckled then said, "Yes, Roman, you're off punishment." "YES!" he whispered, glad that was over. Faye smiled, hearing what he said. After leaving the barbershop with a fresh cut, Roman decided not to go back home but to West Monroe to visit his cousin Drake in "Collegepoint." As he rode down Desiard, he passed ice cream parlors, record shops, and other five and dimes. He passed JJ's Fashions as he neared the Desiard Bridge. Crossing the bridge, he wondered if Drake was home as he entered BC quarters. After reaching Collegepoint, he turned onto Joe Bill Street and pulled into his cousin's driveway where there was a blue Honda parked. "Wonder who that is?" he thought as he turned his bike off. He knocked on the door. The door opened.

"What's up, Man?" Drake asked, happy to see his cousin.

"Chillin," Roman said as they hit each other with a half hug.

"Come in." Drake said, stepping back to let him in and closing the door.

"Where's Aunt Kay?" Man asked as he followed him.

"She and Rick went to New Orleans Thursday," Drake told him. "What? Why didn't you call me?" Roman asked, tripping off just getting this information.

Drake laughed then said, "Yeah right! Aunt Faye had you on lock!" "You got that right!" Roman said as he laughed with him.

"Oh yeah. Say...who's car is that?" Roman asked as they entered the den.

"Oh," he said when he saw the two chicks sitting on the sofa then asked, "What's up?" recovering nicely.

"Hey," they both said with smiles. They were both pretty! One was light-skinned, and the other was brown-skinned.

Drake introduced them: "Man, this is Lisa," he said, pointing at the brown-skinned one, "and this is Trina," he said motioning toward the light-skinned one.

"Nice to meet you," they both said.

"So, what are you to Drake?" Lisa asked.

"I'm his cousin," he told her.

She looked at Trina then said "Oh, We're cousins too. She's visiting from Detroit."

"Is that right? So how do you like Louisiana?" Roman asked.

"It's okay. Just too hot!" she answered. They all shared a laugh. They were having a conversation when Trina got up to go get something out of their car. When she did, Roman looked and thought "Dang! This girl put the 'b' in booty!" She was fine with hazel eyes, a slim waist, and a pretty face. "Detroit's Finest" Roman called her when she came back and their conversation picked up where they left off. As they talked, Roman glanced at Lisa when she said something and noticed her lips. She had sexy ruby red lips.

"Drake will have a good time with those," he thought as she drank her beer leaving lipstick on her glass.

"Do you want something to drink?" Trina asked with a smirk.

He looked at her and laughed.

He saw he was busted by the way she looked at him and said, "Naw, I'm cool," still laughing.

"I bet you are," she said teasingly.

"Very." he replied.

"Hmm, we'll see," she said seductively.

"Roman you wanna roll one?" Drake asked as he kissed Lisa.

"Fo sho," Roman answered.

"Do you ladies smoke?" Roman asked them.

"Fo Sho!" they said mocking him. They all laughed. Roman rolled two, lit one, and passed it to Drake. When it came back to Roman, he blew on the orange heat and told Trina, "Come here." She got up and walked toward him.

"Kneel down," he said. She raised her eyebrows but did what he asked. He placed the joint in his mouth backwards holding it with his teeth then he cupped his hands together and moved toward her placing them around her nose and mouth and blew her a charge.

"I want one" Lisa said, watching her cousin take a charge. Roman motioned for her to come to him and gave her one too. He did this until the joint was gone.

Roman looked at his cousin and asked, "Yo Drake, you got any gin?"

"Yeah. You want some?" Drake responded.

"Yeah" Roman answered, shaking his head. The more they drank, the more they felt their high, which was seen when Drake said, "Lisa, let me holler at chu for a minute" with glazed eyes. She smirked as she reached for his hand and got up. "I'll be back," Drake told his cousin, looking over his shoulder.

"Take your time," Roman said as he and Trina shared a laugh. Trina then got up and came and sat beside him. She started playing in his hair as she asked, "Are you going home?" while looking into his eyes.

"Like this? Naw...I doubt it," he said, smiling as he laid his head back against the sofa and closed his eyes. "Why?" he asked, relaxing. She didn't answer him. She looked at his lips, kissed him, and straddled him in one fluid motion. It took him a few seconds to catch on to what was happening, but when he did, it was on. Slipping her tongue in his mouth, he automatically pulled on it as she grinded in his lap, causing him to come alive. His hardness told her he liked what she was doing. She smiled when she felt it and broke their kiss as she pulled her tank top over her head, looking into his eyes. He leaned forward and unhooked her bra. She slid it off and laid it on the couch. He sat back, admiring her breasts. They were perky and very nice. He wanted to see more.

"Take your shorts off," he whispered. She stood up and did as he asked, wiggling as she pushed them down her hips and over her butt. *This girl is fine*, he thought as he looked at her body and got naked himself.

"Come here," he told her. She came closer and straddled him as they kissed. They explored each other's body as he caressed her breasts and butt and she rubbed her hands up and down his back and slid her hand between his legs and stroked his hardness. He lifted her slightly, and she eased herself down onto his manhood. "You feel good," he told her as she rode him steadily and handled up until they were finished. Afterwards, Roman got up and went to Drake's door.

"Yo Drake" he said as he knocked on the door.

"What's up?" Drake answered.

"What time is Aunt Kay and Rick coming back?" he asked.

"They won't be back til Monday. Why?" he answered.

"I'm spending the night," Roman answered.

"Aight, pull the sofa bed out in the den," Drake answered.

"Bet," he said and went to call his mom.

"Hello?" Faye answered.

"Mom," he started.

"Roman! Where are you?" she said, cutting him off.

"I'm at Drake's house," he told her.

"Oh" she said, calming down wondering where he was.

"Can I spend the night?" he asked her, hoping she would say yes. She paused. "You're just going all out, huh" she said.

"Ma'am?" he said in confusion.

"Nothing. Yes, you can stay, and be careful on that bike," she told him.

He smiled. "Yes ma'am. Thank you, Mama" he answered.

"Call me tomorrow" she told him.

He said, "I will. Bye."

"Bye" she responded and hung up.

He went back into the den, pulled the sofa bed out and laid down with Trina on his chest. She smiled, kissed him, and "not once" did he think about Casey.

CHAPTER V

"Roman!" Faye yelled as she banged on his door again. This was her third time she called his name. Her son had always been a heavy sleeper. She opened the door and turned the light on.

"What?" he snapped, throwing his pillow over his head.

"Boyyy! I know you didn't just snap at me!" she said, frowning as she snatched the pillow off him.

"What is it, Mama?" he groaned, shielding his eyes from the light. "What is it, Mama," she mimicked then added "What it is..." she intoned, "is: you need to get up and come on! I don't have time to wait on you!"

"For what?" he asked, still sleepy.

"Boy!" she snapped, coming closer.

"Okay! Okay! I'm up!" he said, jumping out of his bed and stretched.

She glared at him! "Hurry up, too!" she said and started toward the door.

"Where are we going?" he asked, still stretching.

"To the mall" she answered as she walked out his room.

"Oh," he said. He went into the bathroom, relieved himself, washed his hands and face, brushed his teeth, and went back to his room to get dressed. Ten minutes later, he was ready. He had on a powder blue Nike wind suit with a white t-shirt and some all white Nikes. "Roman! Come on!" his mom yelled.

"Here I come," he said, grabbing his keys and watch from his desk. He walked into the living room where Faye and Isha were waiting on him. They were closing the curtains and blinds. His mom closed the washroom door and turned on the air conditioner. "Let's go!" she said grabbing her keys off the coffee table and heading toward the door not waiting for a response. When he locked the door and got in the car she had already turned the AC on and she and Isha were talking.

"What's up, Ish?" he asked his sister when he closed the car door. "Tired of waiting on you!" she said with an attitude.

He laughed.

She turned around and narrowed her eyes. "You better be glad mama's driving because I would've left you!" and turned back around.

"Yeah right." he said smartly, but knew she was telling the truth. Faye laughed at them as she backed her Continental out of the driveway. She had always wanted one and was glad that she could finally get one. She was thankful for a lot of things and thought about this as they headed to Pecanland Mall. She was at peace, thankful for her marriage, and her children were healthy, well-taken-care-of and blessed. She just hated that they grew up too fast. *One too fast!* she thought as she glanced at Roman in her rearview mirror who was still agitating his sister. Faye was so proud of Isha. She never had to worry about her, and she was graduating this year. She wished she could say the same about Roman, but he was always into something. Frank tries to talk to him but he keeps a lot of things inside just like his dad who thinks that material things are all his kids need instead of more of his time and attention. Ever since he and Jewel had kids, he hadn't been involved in Roman and Isha's life as he had been in the past. The phone calls and trips to California became less frequent. But one thing she could say about Paul is that the money he sends them never stopped. *But that's not all he needs to do* she thought as she looked at the money he sent them in the envelope. She glanced at Isha beside her and admired her daughter's beauty. *She looks like her father but has my hair and skin color* Faye thought as Isha continued to ignore Roman. They argued a lot, but she knew they were tight and loved each other. She pulled into the mall's parking lot and drove around for five minutes before she finally saw a car backing out and waited. She swooped into the parking space and they got out of the car and headed toward the mall. *I hope this doesn't take long*, Faye thought as they made it to the entrance.

"I wonder why they don't have an Oaktree here?" Roman asked Isha standing in Dillards looking at clothes.

She said, "Yeah, like at Fox Hills Mall."

"Yeah or that little shop downtown off Wilshire," he said with a pair of Guess jeans in his hand.

"Look at these prices!" he said.

She looked at the tag and exclaimed, "80 bucks! Tsk! Uh-uh! You only paid $45 for those that you got from that place off Wilshire where you bought your Turkish rope."

"That's the place I was talking about!" he said.

"Well, get used to it because we're not in Los Angeles but in Lou-easy-ana!"

"You heard me," Isha mimicked laughing."

"Fo'sho!" he said, laughing too. Roman had ten pairs of 501's, four pairs of Guess jeans, some other name brand jeans, shirts, t-shirts, and two belts. Isha had a gang of clothes and shoes too. When they were finished, they went to find Faye. She was in the men's department getting some things for Frank. As they approached she turned around and when she saw them she looked at them then the clothes in their hands and asked them, "Do you think you have enough?"

They looked at each other, down at their stuff, and said "Yes ma'am," in unison. She smiled as she thought, *this is why I went back to school! To give them the best with Paul's help! The financial support he gave her for them was a big help!* "Let's go," she told them as she draped Frank's stuff over her arm and they headed toward a cashier. She had already bought most of Isha's stuff and Roman's shoes which were mostly tennis shoes because all he really wore were: Nikes, Filas, K-Swiss, Pumas, and Diadora's. He hated Reeboks, so she never got him those. As they put their stuff on the counter, Faye told the cashier that these would be paid for in cash. "Yes, ma'am," the white female answered politely and rang them up. Roman was checking her out, Faye saw it, and she didn't like it! He saw his mom looking at him and tried to play it off!

"Hmph!" Faye said, narrowing her eyes as she shook her head. "That'll be $1,686 dollars," the cashier said, gaining Faye's attention. She opened the envelope and gave the cashier $1,700 dollars. The cashier counted them, rang it up and gave Faye her change and receipt. "And these will be charged," Faye told her as she put Frank's items on the counter.

"Yes ma'am" she responded and went through the process again. They grabbed all of their packages and got ready to leave after Faye signed her credit card slip and got her receipt

"I'm starving!" Isha said as they walked through the mall.

"Let's eat in the food court," Roman suggested holding all his packages.

"Uh-uh! I'm tired!" Faye said as they walked past Sbarro's. "We'll stop by Popeyes and pick up something," she told them when they reached the car.

"Which one?" Isha asked as they put their stuff in the car.

"Hmm, we could go to the one on Desiard or Renwick Street," Faye said, waiting for a response.

"Naw, mom, let's go to the one on 165 south across from Wossman. It's closer to our house."

"That'll work," Faye said, glad that was settled.

"Hurry up, Roman, and don't slam the trunk," she told him ready to go. The AC was blowing hard as she looked at her watch to check the time. It was 2:25 pm.

"Frank should be up by now," she thought as she backed out and drove off. As soon as she left, another car took that spot. When they entered the house a burst of cool air hit them. Thank God for manufactured air because it was hot outside! Faye went to her bedroom while Isha put the bags from Popeyes on the kitchen counter. Roman was getting all the bags out of the car. He took Isha's stuff to her room and his stuff to his room. He was on his last trip, bringing in the stuff that Faye bought Frank when somebody pulled into his driveway and blew their horn. He turned around and smiled when he saw who it was and asked them to "hold up." He knocked on his mom's bedroom door, put the bags on her sofa, and closed the door. When he turned around, he bumped into Frank. They chuckled as he said, "My bad Frank. What's up?"

"Nothing much. Just enjoying my weekend. What about you?" he asked.

"Nothing much. Bout to go back outside right now. I'll holla at chu later," he told him, rushing to get back outside. Frank laughed as he shook his head, thinking about his stepson. He tightened his robe as he walked into his bedroom where he knew his wife was waiting. "Hey baby," he said when he entered their bedroom and saw her taking off her jewelry and getting undressed.

"Hey honey," she said, smiling as she walked over to him and kissed his lips.

"Mmm, I like that," he said as he watched her with desire.

"How was your day?" she asked.

"Relaxing," he told her, still looking at her body.

"Are you hungry?" she asked.

"For what?" he asked suggestively.

Faye stopped what she was doing and finally looked at her husband, recognizing that tone in his voice and look on his face! He was horny! She blushed but said, "Roman and Isha are here."

He looked disappointed.

"But, we can do something later," she whispered, seductively in his ear as she slid her hand down his chest and stomach.

He shivered as he thought about what they'd do later. "Later," he breathed when she kissed him and left him "happy," closing the door behind her. When she walked into the living room, she saw Isha taking plates out of the cabinet in the kitchen and placing them on the counter.

"Where's Roman?" she asked, looking around as she helped her get the plates ready.

"Outside," Isha said as she reached into the cabinet to get some glasses and placed them on the counter.

"With who?" Faye asked, going into the living room to look out the window. She pulled the curtain back and let it go when she saw who was out there. "So how long have Onika and Casey been out there?" she asked when she walked back into the kitchen.

"Since we made it home," Isha responded.

"Oh. Well, how are you doing?" Faye asked, turning her attention to her daughter and smiling.

Isha returned her smile. "I'm good. Ready to graduate," she said as her mother helped her prepare the plates.
"I'm ready for you to graduate too," Faye said, chuckling as she put dirty rice on the plates then asked, "Did you get the jalapeno peppers out of the fridge yet?"

"No ma'am," Isha answered and stopped what she was doing.

Faye touched her arm and told her, "that's okay. I'll get them. Finish what you're doing" as Frank came into the kitchen.

"Hey Isha," he spoke as he sat down at the counter.

"Hey," she said. Then asked, "Do you want fries or rice?" as she put biscuits on the plate.

"Fries, because I don't like that dirty rice," he answered. She put a sizeable amount of fries on his plate and then asked her mom if she wanted her to go get Roman.

"No. I'll go get him," Faye said as she filled the last glass with ice. When she opened the door to call him, he was gone. She walked back to the kitchen and pulled a chair out so she could sit down. Frank watched her and asked, "What's wrong baby?" recognizing a look of sadness on her face.

"Nothing," she lied and then said, "Roman needs to slow down. We've been gone all day! At least we could eat dinner together." Frank sighed and told her, "Faye, he's a young boy growing up into a young man. Let him live."

She didn't say anything but knew he was right. She got up, put her son's plate in the microwave, his glass of ice in the freezer and sat down to enjoy dinner with them.

"Where's the Suburban?" Roman asked when they pulled into Casey's driveway.

"They went to see our grandmother," Onika told him.

"Oh. Is your sister with them?" he asked.

Onika and Casey looked at each other and burst out laughing.

"Yes Roman! Stacey's with them!" Casey told him, still laughing as she got out of the car.

"Roman, go in the den. The remote's on the mantle over the fireplace," Casey told him when they went in the house and she went to her room. He grabbed the remote and hit the on button as he sat on the couch.

"Casey! I'll be back! I'm going to pick up Nicole!" Onika yelled from the kitchen.

"Okay!" she yelled back.

"See you later, Man," she told him, closing the door before he could respond. He heard the door being locked.

"Casey, do you have anything to drink?" he asked, still trying to find something to watch.

"Ca-" he started to say as he looked toward the dining room and stopped when he saw her standing there with a blanket under her arm butt naked! He was speechless!

"What's wrong?" she asked with a smile on her face.

"Nothing," he said, nodding his head in awe. "Come here," he told her. He couldn't miss her mound that was covered with silky hair as she walked toward him.

"We don't have a lot of time, Roman" she said as she began to spread the blanket out on the carpet. When she turned around, she was surprised but pleased to see him standing there naked too! She smiled. He didn't waste words but took her in his arms and began kissing her lips and feeling on her body. As he guided her to the blanket, he kissed her neck and sucked it gently, then he laid on top of her licking and sucking her breasts.

"Roman," she moaned.

"I know," he mumbled, kissing her breasts and knowing they were pressed for time. He positioned himself over her as she opened her legs wide and planted her feet flat, welcoming him inside. He grabbed his piece and entered her slowly. She was wet and still a tight fit. He slid in and out of her slowly and began to feel more welcomed inside as her walls expanded to accommodate him. She felt good. He began to stroke her harder. He hooked his arms under her legs and put them on his shoulders as he thrusted deeper hitting the bottom. She was enjoying it as he went deeper and told him so as they kept going, trying to get to their destination before anybody came home. They were in sync and after a while, Casey rolled her hips harder and wrapped her arms around his neck, holding him as she started shuddering in ecstasy. Roman kept going. "Cum for me baby," she told him, looking into his eyes, and throwing her hips.

Their rhythm was on. They started going faster and faster and when Roman felt himself about to cum, he pulled out and released the seed all on her stomach and breasts. Knowing they didn't have a lot of time, Casey grabbed a towel and wiped herself off while Roman got dressed.

"You better go," she told him with a kiss.

"I'll call you," he said before closing the door. Casey locked the door, took everything in the bathroom, and jumped in the shower. When Roman was halfway down the block, he saw the Suburban coming down the street. *Just in time,* he thought and smiled when he saw her parents wave at him and Stacey scowling at him in the backseat. He waved back and laughed when Stacey shot him the finger.

~

(Five Months Later)

"I'm tired of you!" Faye shouted in anger.

"But mama-."

"But Mama nothing!" she shouted again. "Every time I look around, I'm dealing with something that's got to do with you!" she shouted again. "I'm tired! I'm tired!" she said as tears filled her eyes and sadness clouded her face. She began to cry! Ever since school started, she had nothing but problems out of Roman! He ditched school, stayed out late, cut classes and never told the truth! His grades were not good! Nothing higher than C's and D's and a few times he tried to forge his progress reports and report cards to pass them off as good grades. But the thing about it is he isn't a dumb child! In fact, he's very smart! She didn't know what to do! *I am too through with him!* she thought as she looked at him through tear-blurred eyes. He knew he'd tripped out. He was tired too! He was tired of people telling him he needed to change and needed to do something with his life! He wanted to make changes in his life but just didn't know how! His mom, along with her mom and relatives

59

even said, "It'll be a miracle if he graduated from high school or made it to his 18th birthday!" They didn't believe in him and he didn't believe in them either! He just didn't care! It was about doing what he wanted to do and enjoying his life!

"Roman?" Faye said, "Roman!" she said louder, interrupting his thoughts.

"Huh?" he said, just realizing she had been talking to him.

"What's on your mind?" she asked, sniffling and wiping her nose and eyes.

"Nothing." he lied.

She dropped her head and let out a lengthy breath, exasperated. She raised her head looking at him with fresh tears and said, "Well, you know you will have to go to Monroe City School Board and see Superintendent Starks to get reinstated in school.

He blew out a deep breath and said, "I know."

"I'll call today and make an appointment," she said as she went into the kitchen to get a glass of water. She came back into the living room, sat on the couch and asked again, "Roman, how could you do that to that girl?"

He took a deep breath. "Mama, I told you it was an accident," he told her, tired of repeating himself.

"How?" she asked.

He sighed then told her, "A few of us were standing around outside in front of the school kickin' it and there were some girls with us and I'm known to play jokes. Well… I had a box of matches and I was striking them and throwing them at the girls just joking around and we all thought it was funny, until one of the matches landed in one girl's hair that had a curl and it started smoking! When I saw it, I ran over there and started patting her hair to put it out and make sure she didn't get burned! She wasn't hurt, and it didn't burn her because I moved fast, but she told the principal and he expelled me."

Faye sighed and shook her head as she said, "Don't you know you could've hurt that girl, Roman? What were you thinking?"

"I know, Mama! I know! I messed up!" He told her, tired of going over the same thing. He was sorry for what he'd done but couldn't change it and talking about it surely wouldn't change it, but Faye wasn't finished.

She sighed then told him, "You need to make some changes! I'm tired of this and this isn't the first time you've been expelled!"

He looked at her, not believing she was bringing that up again!

"Yes I'm bringing it up," she said as if reading his thoughts then said, "You got expelled for being drunk on campus and I got you back in then you got expelled for fighting and I got you back in. Well, this time that's a wrap! When I get you back in this time, stay in because this is your last year here!" His eyes widened! Faye continued: "When school is out, you're gonna be on a plane on the first thing smoking to LA!"

"What?" he said stunned!

"You heard me! I'm calling your dad to let him know!" she told him as she stood up and walked out of the living room tired of talking to him and with her mind made up! Roman couldn't believe it but knew that was the end of the discussion!

Ringgg! Ringgg! "Hello?" she said as she put her keys and purse on the counter. Roman walked right past her and went to his room. "Yes, he is. Hold on, " Faye said. "Roman! Telephone!" she told him, waiting for him to pick up.

"I got it!" he told her and said, "hello?"

Faye hung up when she heard him say hello.

"Heyyy! What are you doing?" Casey asked, wondering if he had already been to the superintendent's office.

"Nothing. Just pissed off! I just got back," he told her, exhaling loudly and rubbing his forehead as he lay in his bed thinking about it.

"And?" she asked.

"And, I got back in. He paddled me three times with a fiberglass paddle on the back of my thighs as I leaned forward in front of his desk."

"Ohhh!" he heard her say.

"I know right and it hurt like a mug too!" he told her, remembering the pain.

"I'm sorry baby," she said softly.

"Yeah, me too, but at least I'm back in school" he said.

"I love you," she told him.

"I love you too but listen, I'm about to take a nap because I'm tired," he told her while yawning.

"Okay." she said.

"I'll call you later because I'm not grounded. I guess mom felt that the paddling was punishment enough," he told her, turning to his side.

"All right. Talk to you later. Bye," she told him.

"Later" he said and hung up.

~

"You're out of control!" somebody yelled as he walked the hall to his English class. People laughed, but it didn't bother him. He knew that he had messed up, but that episode was over with: cancelled! When he walked into the classroom, he saw the girl whose hair almost caught on fire. He sat down next to her and put his books on his desk.

"Can I talk to you?" he asked, turning toward her, waiting for her to look at him as he looked at her hair. She looked at him and sighed. "Roman, I really don't-" she said, but Roman held up his hands and said, "five minutes. That's all I want."

She finally looked in his eyes and nodded her head okay.

"I'm sorry about what happened and I want you to know that I would never have intentionally done that to you! It scared me and I know it scared you! It scared all of us! It was an accident!" They held each other's gaze until she looked away.

Finally, she looked at him again and sighed saying "Roman, I know you were just playing around and I know that we all thought what you were doing was funny but when my hair almost caught on fire, it was no longer funny!"

"I -" he started.

"Let me finish!" she said, cutting him off, "Roman, I thought I was about to die! I was so afraid," she said as her bottom lip started trembling and tears filled her eyes.

"Hey," he said leaning forward and touching her on her shoulder to comfort her, but she dropped her head and smiled through her tears as she said "I'm okay. I'm just glad I'm not hurt and, Roman, I'm sorry I got you in trouble. I panicked," she added, lifting her head and looking at him.

"Hey! We're cool and that episode is cancelled! I'm just glad you're all right!" he said, holding his fist out for her to "knock that down" and she did just as people started coming into the classroom.

~

She was walking down the hall going to her next class. She had a lot on her mind and was deep in thought when she heard somebody loudly say: "There she is right there!" She looked back to see who it was and what was going on.

"Felicia!" she said through gritted teeth when she saw her and her crew! They were pointing at her too, but she kept walking.

"Here I am minding my business and this girl is trying to mess with me!" she mumbled to herself in anger. Everybody was looking, but she kept walking because she was passing the principal's office and wanted nothing to jump off there because graduation was too close! She went through the doors, entering the school lobby. They were right behind her now because just as the doors closed they opened again!

"Hey! Hey!" Felicia yelled. "You hear me talking to you tramp!" she told her.

"Ohhh!" people said when they heard the diss, wondering if they would see a fight. She stopped and turned around because she was tired of this heifer!

"What's your problem!" Isha snapped, adjusting her purse.

"You know what my problem is, trick!" she told her, rolling her neck and pointing her finger in Isha's face.

"Uh-uh! Hold up!" Isha said, taking a step back and telling her "Don't you ever put your finger in my face!"

"I can put my finger wherever I want to!" Felicia told her as she and her crew took a step toward her.

"Naw! You're a lie! Not with me!" Isha told her tiring of going back and forth. Stacey, Casey, and a few of their homegirls were laughing and talking as they entered the lobby and noticed the crowd. They went to see what was going on. As they got closer, they heard females arguing. Casey saw one of the girl's hair and skin color and recognized her instantly!

"Girl, that's Isha! Come on!" she said urgently to Stacey, grabbing her arm pushing through the crowd with their friends.

"Leave my man alone!" Felicia yelled, getting bolder because of her crew and the crowd!

"Tsk! I don't want your man! What you need to do is keep your man on a leash! Oh, and just so you know, he wouldn't ever stand a chance with me!" Isha told her and turned to walk away.

"Ohhh" people said and burst out laughing.

Felicia, embarrassed and angry, ran and pushed Isha in her back! Isha stumbled, regained her balance, quickly turned around, and dropped her purse, spurring her!

Her crew was about to jump in when Casey short stopped them and said, "I wish y'all would! Come on!" posting up on them.

"This ain't cho business!" one of them said.

"It is now! What's up!" Stacey yelled as she and her friends stood beside Casey waiting for them to say something stupid! They didn't. They just watched as their friend fought and she was getting dealt with too! She was no match for Isha! Isha kept hitting her, thinking about what Roman told her!

"Hit em' hard! Hit em' fast! Don't let up! And whatever you do, don't put your head down!" Girls have a habit of doing that and you can't hit what you can't see! Now she saw why he told her that when she spurred Felicia! As soon as she hit her, Felicia closed her eyes and put her head down and she went to work! Isha hit her with lefts, rights and uppercuts!

"Teacher!" somebody yelled! Everybody started scattering! Somebody grabbed Felicia, Casey grabbed Isha, and one of Stacey's friends grabbed Isha's purse as they ran into the auditorium.

"Go backstage! Hurry up!" Stacey yelled as they ran down the aisle and up the stairs behind the curtains! They were trying to catch their breath as their hearts raced!

"Here's your purse." one of them said, handing it to Isha.

"Thank you," Isha then said, "You play basketball right?"

"Yeah," she answered and said smiling, "Say, you got a nice squabble game."

Isha shook her head as she thought about it and said, "I didn't wanna fight but that heifer pushed me."

"Well, she won't be pushing you no mo'!" Stacey said matter-of-factly. They laughed.

"Girlll! I felt sorry for her," Casey said, "but then I was like...nah, handle that heifer, Isha!" They laughed harder!

"What I don't understand," one of them said seriously, "Is why would she pick a fight with you if she knew that she couldn't fight?" and shook her head as they laughed.

"Because she thought I couldn't fight," Isha answered.

"She thought wrong!" Casey said, still laughing.

"Plus she had her crew with her" somebody else said.

"Speaking of that, I appreciate y'all lookin' out for me," Isha told them.

They said, "no problem and you're welcome."

"Hey! How did you learn how to fight?" Stacey asked.

"My brother Roman taught me," Isha told her and appreciated it. "Oh. Well, we might as well stay here until the bell rings," Stacey said, changing the subject. They all agreed and talked for the next 30 minutes.

"What's up?" Roman said, bursting into Isha's room.

"Roman! I've told you about coming into my room without knocking!" She told him, raising up her head and scowling at him. He ignored her and asked, "uh-uh. What happened today?"

She shook her head and asked, "Who told you?" as she raised up on her elbows and looked at him.

"I took Casey home today. That's how," he told her.

"I should've known," she said, smiling as she thought about what Casey, Stacey, and their friends did today.

"What are you smiling about?" he asked looking at her puzzled. "Nothing," she told him, not wanting to tell him.

"Well, it's all over school and Felicia had to go home so she wouldn't get in trouble," he said plopping down on her bed and laying beside her.

"She was pretty banged up," he told her then asked, "Who taught you how to fight?"

"My mama!" she said with a smirk and laughed.

"What!" he said, jumping up and throwing punches. "I taught you how to fight, girl! Isha Ali!" he shouted as he threw a combination and put his hands up in victory.

"You stupid!" she told him, laughing as he continued.

He laughed too and sat down beside her. "But seriously, I'm glad you're all right. You handled your business," he told her, giving her a quick hug and stood up saying, "okay! Enough of this bonding. I'm about to go shower. Time and Chance, baby," he said, holding his fist out for her to knock it down.

"Time and Chance," she repeated as she held her fist out and knocked it down. As they grew up, this was a scripture they shared with each other: Ecclesiastes 9:11.

CHAPTER VI

As Roman walked to his class, his mind drifted to Casey. She had been acting distant since he'd told her about his mom sending him to California.

"Hey Roman," a female spoke as they passed each other.

"What's up," he said distractedly. He couldn't put his finger on it but something was off. But he also knew not to trip because a female will do what she wants to do. *Bet*, he said to himself as he entered the science building to go to his chemistry class. He liked chemistry and found it to be easy. *In fact, he found a lot of his classes easy when he attended*, he thought as he walked up the stairs. When he made it to the classroom and walked in the door, he noticed a substitute teacher and immediately said, "Oh, my bad. Wrong class" and turned around and walked right back out. He heard some laughs as he left. He was thinking about where he could go as he walked back down the stairs. He walked out of the building and toward the gym. It was cold outside, so the doors were closed but he knew they were not locked. The heat hit him as he opened the door into the gym's lobby. He looked through the window of the gym door and saw the fellas playing basketball and the females playing volleyball. As he did, he noticed Charlene watching the fellas play. He licked his lips as he scanned her body, paying close attention to her hips, butt, and legs. She was fine and looked like a chocolate doll with that smooth dark skin, silky long hair and pretty dark eyes. She turned around and walked to the bleachers to sit down and when she did those shorts she had on got his attention because of her walk! She had the walk that when she did all you could think about was *how it would feel to have her in bed. That Nasty Walk and she knew it too!* he thought as she sat down. She flipped her hair out of her face as she continued to watch the fellas play. She leaned back against the bleacher, resting her head on her hand as she put her elbow on the bleacher, looking bored. She scanned the gym, looking at people do their thing as she did nothing. As he watched her she sighed, glanced at the door and did a "double take" when she saw him! He smiled, and she smiled as he backed away from the door to wait. She got up and tugged on her shorts as she walked toward the door.

"Hey," she said softly with a smile when she closed the door.

"Hey. What's up Char?" he said, leaning against the wall with his right foot on the wall.

"Nothing," she said in her soft, sexy voice.

"You look good. Come here," he told her, smiling and motioning for her with his finger. She "tsked" as she walked over to him and leaned her right shoulder against the wall, folding her arms across her chest as she faced him.

"What are you doing in here?" she asked him.

"Coming to see you," he told her.

"Yeah right," she said, not believing him.

"Seriously," he told her.

She sighed and said, "Roman don't lie," shaking her head.

"I'm not," he told her.

"Let you tell it. Whatever," she told him.

"Would I lie to you?" he asked .

"Well-" she started but stopped as he pushed himself off the wall, ran his hand down her cheek and kissed her lips as he looked into her eyes. He whispered things in her ears he knew she wanted to hear. He slid his hands down her back and rested them on her butt. She shivered and bit her bottom lip, liking his touch.

He kissed her again and said, "Well?" as he caressed her face.

She looked into his eyes and asked, "How's your girlfriend?"

"Is that a factor?" he asked her cooly, still caressing her face. She tried to avert her eyes, but he lifted her chin, looking into her eyes and asked, "Is it?" He knew it wasn't but wanted her to say it. He knew she still wanted him and *today* she would in one way at least. "You know it isn't," she answered, relenting as she kissed him and closed her eyes. She missed him so much! As they kissed, she felt the heat rising between them and his hardness too! He touched her breast, and a moan escaped her lips as she rubbed his back. He broke their kiss, took her right hand, and walked toward the girl's restroom in the lobby.

She hesitated saying, "Roman?" with a questioning look on her face.

"It's cool. Trust me," he told her with a smile. She did, and they walked into the restroom. He locked the door, and she pulled her shorts and panties down, taking one leg out as he unbuckled his belt and pulled his pants and boxers down. She watched him as he stroked his piece. She kissed him, turned around and put her hands on the sink waiting for him. He put a hand on her waist, placed his piece near her opening and was surprised how wet she was as he slowly entered her and remembered how good she felt when he was inside her. As he held her hips, she slowly pushed back on him. He pushed all the way inside of her as she rolled her hips. He stroked her slowly as she continued to roll her hips with his hands on her waist. She met every stroke in a perfect rhythm as their bodies continued to become one. They were enjoying each other as he thrust deeper inside of her. She missed him and wanted this moment to last because she still loved him. Even though she knew he didn't love her, she still gave herself to him because he was good! She understood the game but didn't care. These were her thoughts until she felt an orgasm coming and quickly told him, "Don't move!" He did, and she worked her hips, rolling and pushing back on him like she wanted as she got closer! He was getting close too! As she felt herself begin to cum, her knees buckled but she kept going as he grabbed her hips and began to cum and he came hard too, grunting and sounding like something primitive! She rolled her hips until he went limp. She turned around, kissed him, and they got dressed. She walked out of the restroom and stood there to make sure nobody was around before he came out. She knocked on the door and he came out.

"Know what?" he said.

"What?" she said.

"I smell like sex!" he told her. They laughed.

"It was good! You were good!" she told him.

"I know," he said nonchalantly.

"Shut up! You're still conceited!" she said as she laughed and hit his arm. He laughed too, and they continued to talk.

He looked at his watch and said, "I gotta go. It's almost time for the bell to ring."

She looked at her watch and told him, "Me too because I have to go shower and get dressed!"

He took her hand, kissed her and told her, "Okay. I'll see you later." "All right," she said. After he left, she looked at her watch and rushed into the gym to shower and dress before the bell rang! "Hmph, wonder where she's been?" Stacey thought as Charlene rushed past her going toward the locker room but quickly went back to her conversation. *IF SHE ONLY KNEW!*

~

They'd been gone all day and now Casey and Onika sat in the den eating Mickey D's and Wendy's while Nicole was enjoying herself and making a mess of her "happy meal," but they didn't notice because they were having a conversation and enjoying their food.

"I can't believe Man is really going to California to stay," Onika said as she took a bite of her double cheeseburger.

"Me either," Casey said as she dipped some fries in ketchup. Feeling hurt and disappointed, Casey said, "but it's not his choice," as she ate her fries.

Onika shook her head and asked, "What happened?" before taking another bite of her burger. Casey was still chewing and held up her finger, letting Onika know to wait as she drank some soda.

"Ahh!" she said savoring the soda and told her, "He got expelled during the first semester of school and his mom was pissed!"

Onika frowned and said, "But he got back in and that was months ago!"

"I know, but she doesn't care!" Casey told her.

"That's too strong!" Onika said, shaking her head in disbelief. Casey started thinking about being without Roman and stopped eating.

Onika looked at her and asked "You're gonna miss him, huh?" Casey looked at her, nodded her head and then said, "Yeah and I don't know if I can handle a long-distance relationship."

She paused then said, "I can try but I really don't know."

Onika looked at her then asked her, "You do know he loves you right?"

Casey sighed and instead of answering just burst out laughing! Onika frowned in confusion. Casey pointed past her as she laughed! "Girl, look at Nicole!" she said, still laughing!

"Nicole!" she exclaimed when she turned around and saw her daughter! Nicole looked up when she heard her name and when she did Onika couldn't help but laugh too! Nicole had ketchup and mustard all on her cheeks, face, shirt and hands, a French fry in her hair and a pickle on her shirt! She was a mess! She looked at her mother and auntie with her little face full of ketchup and mustard, trying to figure out what was so funny. Casey couldn't stop laughing!

"Shut up, Casey! Don't laugh at my baby!" Onika told her as she reached out to her daughter and told her "Come here, baby! Let mama clean you up!" Nicole let go of the hamburger bun she was holding and reached for her mom. She smiled when Onika picked her up. "Stop laughing at my baby, Casey!" Onika said as she took Nicole to the bathroom.

"I'm trying!" Casey said, still laughing. She finally stopped and went back to eating, but when her mind drifted back to Roman, she lost her appetite. They had been together almost a year, and she wanted it to be more, but how could they be with him in California! She loves him and just couldn't believe he was leaving, but she was also thinking about something else. A guy named Craig Hill was throwing her action, and he had just moved to their neighborhood. "Hmm," she said, thinking. He moved into the neighborhood and Roman is moving away, so could this be a sign that she should get with Craig and let Roman go? She thought he was cute and didn't want to admit it, but why not with Roman leaving! Roman knows him too! In fact, she had seen Roman over his house on Vegas Drive when she and her mom were going to the store. She didn't know what to do, but one thing was for sure she was in confusion.

"Girl-I-surrender-cause I'm taking a fall/Come get it baby-you can have it all." Roman liked this song by The Deele and said, "not bad" to himself as he sat in the auditorium at talent show practice, bobbing his head listening to these boys jam. He knew all of them. Gerald, Cotton, Trey, Frost, Jason, and Craig. The music and their vocals were tight, but that's what set Carroll High School's talent shows apart from all others. They didn't use performance tapes because the band director got the sheet music for each song and had a live band play it. Roman was up next and he was doing "Wild and Loose" by The Time with Gerald, Cotton, and Trey. Going over the lyrics in his head, he glanced to his right and saw Casey. He raised his eyebrows when he noticed the look in her eyes and the object of her attention: Craig Hill and she was looking at him like she wanted him to be her man or like he was her man.

"Hmm" he said then thought about one thing his dad taught him was: *don't ever trip over a woman because there are too many out there, so, when one is gone, another will come along.* He looked at Craig and couldn't help but shake his head as he thought about how he took him under his wing and put him down with him, Gerald, Cotton, and Trey. He taught him how to talk, walk, dress and other things and Casey seemed to be choosing him. *Imagine that,* he said and laughed to himself. Casey was chillin' with Stacey and their crew. She felt Roman looking at her but didn't look his way. Roman turned his attention back to the stage. He respected the game and didn't hate the playa or the game because Casey had a right to choose whoever she wanted to, but this was about respect. *Cool,* he thought as the song grew to a close. He felt someone staring at him and when he looked it was Stacey. He nodded his head at her and she looked toward the stage, pointed at Craig, pointed at Casey, grinned, and waved at Roman mouthing "Bye-bye." Casey couldn't see her because Stacey was sitting behind her in the second row. Stacey was out of control! He knew how to handle her, though! He licked his lips and flicked his tongue, imitating oral sex. She was shocked! Her mouth dropped open, and she turned her attention back to the stage! He couldn't help it! He laughed out loud! Some people looked at him, including Casey, but he didn't care. When the song ended, they announced that he was next, and he walked over and spoke to Casey and her friends. They returned his greeting, then he spoke to Stacey.

"What's up, Stace?" he asked, smirking.

"Not you!" she mumbled, rolling her eyes at him.

He smiled and went up on stage. He spoke to the fellas one by one with Craig being last.

"What up, Craig?" he asked him with a half hug and handshake. "Coolin'," he responded.

"Straight. That track was tight," Roman told him.

"'Preciate it, Man," Craig said.

Roman turned his attention to his boys Gerald, Cotton, and Trey and asked, "Y'all ready?"

"You know it," they responded.

"Bet," he told them.

"Yo Craig, come here for a minute," he said before he made it down the stairs.

Craig walked over to him. "What's up?" he asked.

"Nothing much," Roman said, putting his arm around Craig's shoulder and looking him in his eyes. Then he asked him, "Would you do me a favor?" as he looked at him and then at Casey.

Craig knitted his brow as he asked, "What's up?"

Roman smiled and pointed at Casey as he said, "Go chill with my girl and take care of her for me. She likes you.

This caught him off guard and all he could say was, "huh?" because, truth be told, he liked her and wanted to get with her but didn't want Man to know it. Casey and her crew watched the exchange wondering what was going on and their question was answered when Craig came and sat down beside Casey.

"What did he tell you?" she asked, not even looking at him. He told her while she kept her eyes on Roman, watching him intently as she felt the sting of what he'd just done!

One of Stacey's friends whispered, "Oh no, he didn't!" thinking to herself that Roman was tripping because Casey had just told her she thought Craig was cute and she kind of liked him.

Stacey heard everything and was pissed! She shook her head thinking, "He just put his boy in the car with my sister in front of her friends trying to pass her off as if she was nothing! I'll be so glad when he's gone!" The sound of music interrupted her thoughts, and she looked at Roman with anger as they performed the song they were doing! After their song, the band director gave them the order of the show and told them to be in the auditorium at 5 o'clock pm before everybody got ready to leave. Roman went to get his stuff and prepared to leave.

Casey called his name: "Roman."

He turned around and asked, "What's up, baby? Do you need a ride home?"

She just looked at him, and he held her gaze. She shook her head and answered, "No. Onika is coming to pick me and Stacey up. Do you want me to call you when I get home?" she asked him.

He said, "that's cool," then walked over and kissed her.

She broke the kiss and told him, "Okay. I'll call you later. Bye." "Bye," he replied and walked away. When he was gone, she licked her lips savoring the flavor of the candy he had in his mouth when they kissed which was now in hers.

"Hello?" Isha answered, ready to get back to her conversation. "Hey Isha. This is Casey. Is Roman there?" she asked.

"Heyy. Yeah, he's here, but he's in the shower right now. I can tell him to call you when he gets out though," she told her.

"Okay, that's fine," she replied.

"Alright. Bye-bye" Isha answered before hanging up. Casey wondered what kind of conversation they would have when he called her back.

"Casey, are you gonna talk to man tonight?" Onika asked her as she walked into her room.

Casey looked up and said, "yeah, why?"

Onika said, "Because I need a favor, so when you talk to him let him know I need to talk to him."

"Okay," she said.

After her sister left her mind went right back to Roman and what happened today. She was thinking about what she would say when the phone rang.

Ringgg! Ringgg! It startled her! She turned over and reached for her phone.

"Hello?" she said.

"What's up? Isha told me you called," he said, and despite herself, she smiled when she heard his voice. She was still mad at him though.

"Yeah, I did. I'm glad you called," she told him as she twirled the cord on her phone.

"Oh, yeah?" he answered.

"Yeah. Roman, when are you leaving?" she said, getting right to the point.

"My mom told me at the end of May or the first week of June," he told her then asked

"Are you gonna miss me?" she said with emotion in her voice. "Yeah!" he told her, then asked a question of his own.

"Are we gonna stay together through the long distance?"

Silence.

"You there?" he asked.

"Yeah. I'm here" she told him then said, "Roman, I've never been in a long-distance relationship, so I don't know if I can handle it". "Well, check this out, let's try and see what happens," he told her. "All right," she said, not wanting to talk about it anymore. She really wanted to talk to him about what happened today but didn't want to argue with him. They continued to talk, and she remembered something!

"Oh yeah! Onika wants to talk to you about something."

"All right, put her on the phone," he told her.

"Hold on! She told him, then shouted, "Onika!"

"Yeah!" her sister shouted back.

"Man's on the phone!" Casey said.

"Okay!" her sister said, heading her way.

"Here she is," Casey told him, giving her the phone.

"Hey," Onika said.

"What's up?" he asked.

"Smashing for gas" she told him.

He looked at his clock and said, "It's kind of late right now."

"Naw, not tonight. Tomorrow," she said quickly.

"All right, 6 o'clock cool?" he asked.

"Yeah," she said.

"All right. Later," he told her ready to talk back to Casey.

"Later," she told him and told Casey thanks after giving her the phone back and walking out.

"I see," Casey said when she put the phone to her ear.

"Don't trip," he told her.

"I'm not. Just be careful," she told him.

"Don't I always." he said smartly.

"See Roman! I'll talk to you later!" she said in anger.

"Okay. I'm tired anyway, he told her then added, oh and Casey," sounding like he'd forgotten something.

"What Roman!" she quipped.

"I love you," he told her. She laughed thinking, *he always knows what to say!*

"You're a trip but I love you too!" she said, still laughing.

He said, "Good night," and she did the same.

~

"What's up?" he said as Onika got out of her car.

"Being on time," she told him as she gave him a screwdriver and got in the passenger seat. He walked to the back of her car, took her license plate off and got in the driver's seat. They pulled up to a gas pump and Roman got out, leaving the car's engine running. He pulled his hat down, took the gas cap off and began pumping gas. When he was finished, he jumped back in the car and took off! He hit two turns, drove down some street into a neighborhood, and pulled into a driveway. He got out and put her license plate back on as Onika got out and got in the driver's seat. When he was finished, a light came on in the driveway.

A door opened and an older-looking woman looked out and asked, "Who are you looking for?"

Roman pretended to look at a piece of paper in his hand as he said, "I got the wrong address. I'm sorry. I thought this was 506, but this is 501." She looked at him, nodded her head when he smiled and closed her door.

As she drove, Onika glanced at him and smiled as she said, "You think fast on your feet."

"Sometimes you have to," he told her, looking like something was on his mind and it made her wonder if something was wrong. He was quiet.

At a red light she told him, "Roman, I hate you're leaving. You're a cool person, you're like a brother to me, and you treat my sister right."

"Yeah, you're cool too. You wanna know something?" he asked looking at her.

"What?" she asked.

"The light's green" he told her, nodding toward the light. Somebody blew their horn as she looked at the light and pulled off laughing with Roman, who was laughing at her as she drove.

When they hit Century Boulevard she asked, "Are you coming to my house or going home?"

"Home. I can't deal with your sister Stacey tonight! I don't know what it is about me she doesn't like and I don't care!" he told her with a lot on his mind. She understood. She turned left on

Oregon Trail and went around the loop to make a circle. She made a right on Nevada Drive and pulled into his driveway. He grabbed his hat and told her to tell Casey to call him.

"Okay and thanks for the gas," she told him before he got out.

"No problem. Be safe," he told her and closed the door. She drove off when he walked into his house.

~

Isha was walking to her next class talking and laughing with some friends and she was excited because graduation was in two months! "No More School!" Freedom!

They were walking past the guidance office when Mrs. Bragg, the junior and senior guidance counselor said, "Ms. Chance, I need to see you in my office, please" and walked back into her office.

She and her friends exchanged a glance and Isha just shrugged and told them, "I don't know. I'll catch up with y'all later."

"All right," they said, walking off and resuming their conversation. Isha turned around and went to Mrs. Braggs's office, wondering what this was about because she knew she had enough credits to graduate.

"Have a seat," Mrs. Braggs told her when she entered her office. She also closed a folder on her desk with Isha's name on it when she sat down. Isha adjusted her bookbag and purse.

Mrs. Bragg picked the folder up on her desk and flipped through it as she said, "I was going over your file and I didn't see any choices for college. Any reason why? What do you plan on doing after high school?" she asked, looking at her over her glasses.

"Oh, I haven't decided yet, but college isn't one of them," Isha told her and glanced at her watch.

Mrs. Bragg sighed then said, "Isha, you're a smart girl!"

"You took the ACT and got a good score! Why wouldn't you pursue college? What's wrong?" she asked.

I can't tell you. In fact, I can't tell anybody, Isha thought as she tried to keep a straight face. She sighed and said, "Mrs. Bragg, nothing is wrong. I just want to wait for a while and enjoy the freedom I'll have not going to school before I make a decision. I mean, I wouldn't have to go in the fall. I could go in the spring." Isha hoped she believed her, but Mrs. Bragg studied her because she'd known Isha and her bad brother since she was a freshman and there was something she wasn't telling her but she wouldn't push.

She sighed and told her in frustration, "Isha, I advise against it because I care about you but as you said it is your choice even though I wish you would reconsider because there are colleges that would love to have you as a student." That hurt! But Isha didn't have a choice! This was how it would be, and she hoped she would respect it! She stood up and placed her bookbag and purse on her shoulder.

"Mrs. Bragg, I need to go," she told her.

"Okay," she said as she stood up too and surprised Isha when she came from behind her desk and hugged her telling her, "Everything will be all right." Isha hugged her back tight, needing that and when they released each other there were tears in her eyes.

"Thank you," Isha said.

"You're welcome" Mrs. Bragg told her and watched her walk out.

"Defense! *Clap! Clap!* Defense! *Clap! Clap!*" the cheerleaders cheered as the Carroll Bulldogs varsity basketball team tried to keep their opponent the West Monroe Rebels from scoring! It was a tight game! The Rebels were up 71-69 with a few minutes left in the 4th quarter. Isha, Roman, their cousin Farrah and her friend Jennifer were sitting together watching the game. Jennifer is Farrah's best friend. She's a former Carroll High student who transferred to a magnet school in Lafayette because of her academics. She had finished her finals early, so she came to kick it with Farrah. She missed her a lot! They had a lot of catching up to do and it would've been easier if she would keep her eyes off Roman! She remembered him as a freshman but really didn't pay any attention to him but now was a different story! She thought he was fine, and he was confident and sexy!

She had been wondering if he was seeing anybody and decided to ask, "so Roman, what are you now, a sophomore?" she asked, looking at him with her beautiful green eyes.

"Yeah," he answered, absently focusing on the game. Isha and Farrah both looked at each other and raised their eyebrows thinking the same thing: *Was she trying to come on to Roman?*

"Hmph," Isha mumbled, shaking her head slightly.

"Sooo, where's your girlfriend?" she asked casually, hoping he didn't have one!

Isha looked and whispered to Farrah, "She is coming on to him! She is out of control!"

"Yeah!" Man yelled, suddenly jumping up when Carroll scored! He was whistling and clapping with the rest of the home fans! Jennifer felt ignored!

She grew impatient and said his name: "Roman!" while brushing her blonde hair out of her face.

"What? Oh, she's on the visitor's side," he told her, giving her his attention as he sat back down. Isha and Farrah looked on and shook their heads thinking *he must be slippin' if he doesn't see what's going on but he did!* He was just playing her like he wasn't interested! Back in the day, she wouldn't give him no play but now was a different story! *My how things change!* he thought as he looked at her and had to admit that she is an attractive white girl and her body is really nice! She looked like that white chick from that singing group that he couldn't remember the name of right now.

"Oh," she said, sounding disappointed but then got bold and asked, "Does she make you happy?"

"Fo'sho!" he said smiling. "What about you? Is anybody making you happy?" he asked.

"No, not yet," she told him, smiling and feeling like this was beginning to go her way.

"Hmm, maybe that'll change," he said nonchalantly.

She smiled and said coyly, "I hope so," causing him to smile too. "Ahem!" Isha cleared her throat and asked them, "Are y'all ready to go because the game is over?" emphasizing it by waving her hands at people beginning to leave. They all laughed and got up to leave too. When they made it outside, they continued to talk and wait out the crowd. They were talking about how Carroll came back and won the game with a minute left in the game when Casey and her homegirl Tanjee came up to them.

"Hey baby," Casey said as she walked up, kissed Roman, and spoke to everyone else, hugging Isha in the process.

"What's up, homegirl?" he asked Tanjee, hugging her.

"Nothing much. I just hate that we lost," she told him, frowning. "Well, you know you could always come back to the CHS," he told her, spreading his arms out wide.

"Shut up, Roman!" she told him as everybody laughed.

"So baby, are you coming with us?" Casey asked as she hugged his waist and looked up at him.

"Yeah. That's cool," he told her, then told Farrah to take care of Isha.

"All right," she said just as Isha said, "Tsk! Boy, please! Bye!" and rolled her eyes. They laughed!

"It was nice seeing you, Roman," Jennifer told him.

"Same here" he responded. They all said their goodbyes and began to go their separate ways.

"I gotta watch that heifer!" Casey thought as they were leaving and when she turned around she noticed Jennifer watching Roman! "Trick!" she said under breath.

Jennifer was spending the weekend with Farrah. They had gone to the kettle after the game and had just dropped Isha off.

"So Farrah, what's up with your cousin?" Jennifer asked as they headed to Farrah's house.

"What do you mean?" Farrah asked, playing like she didn't know what she was talking about as they rode down 165 South.

"Well, is he serious about that chick or what?" she asked, making her position clear.

"I don't know-" she started to say but Jennifer cut her off.

"You should-" she began but Farrah cut her off saying, "If you would let me finish! Dang!" Jennifer turned in her seat and looked toward her, waiting.

Farrah changed lanes to take the next exit and told her, "I don't know, but I don't think it'll last and in fact I know it won't last!" Jennifer's green eyes gleamed as she listened to her and asked, "How do you know?"

"Because he's going to California in a few weeks to stay with his dad."

"For real!" she said as Farrah turned into her driveway and parked under the carport.

"Come on," Farrah told her, ignoring her stare as she grabbed her purse and got out of the car. She unlocked the door, and they went straight to her bedroom, being careful not to wake her parents and brothers. Jennifer plopped down on Farrah's bed and sat Indian style as she watched Farrah and waited for her to continue as she closed the door. She didn't but undressed as she stood in front of her mirror and noticed Jennifer looking at her. She tried to ignore her but Jennifer kept looking at her until she laughed and turned around asking, "What?" holding her palms out.

"You know what!" Jennifer told her, narrowing her eyes.

Farrah kept laughing but finally said, "okay! Okay, what do you want to know?"

"I want to know how long he is staying," she said.

"I believe forever," Farrah told her as she put on a pair of shorts and a t-shirt to sleep in.

"For real?" Jennifer said disappointed.

"Yeah. He's going to school there in the fall. I believe at Crenshaw," Farrah told her, nodding her head and sitting down on her bed. Jennifer got quiet and sat there looking like she had something on her mind and then smiled.

"Hey! Do you have the address where he'll be staying?" she asked as her wheels turned!

Farrah furrowed her brow and asked, "Yeah, why?"

Jennifer looked at her with a smile and sang, "Because, I wanna write to him!" as she stood up and started getting undressed too. "What for?" Farrah asked, confused.

"So we can keep in touch!" Jennifer told her looking in the mirror at Farrah.

"But!" Farrah said as Jennifer cut her off and turned around saying "Don't worry! I got this!" smiling mischievously with her green eyes gleaming!

Farrah was tired, so she said, "Okay. I'll give you the address in the morning."

"And the phone number!" Jennifer added.

Farrah sighed. "And the phone number. In the morning. Now turn out the light!" Farrah told her ready to go to sleep.

"Cool!" Jennifer said and did what she asked.

"Where are you going, Roman?" Casey snapped as he got up to leave!

"Home!" he said looking at her in anger! He had been in the den with her and Tanjee, laughing and talking. Well, at least he and Tanjee had until Casey started tripping! She had been kind of quiet and he got tired of trying to find out what was wrong and then it came out! She was tripping about Farrah's friend Jennifer!

He looked at Tanjee and his face softened as he told her, "I'll see you later."

She looked up at him and told him, "all right. Be cool," feeling uneasy in this situation with them arguing.

"Roman!" Casey hissed as he walked out the door with her right behind him! "Roman!" she said again, grabbing his arm!

He stopped and asked her in anger, "What? What Casey?"

"I'm sorry," she said wrapping her arms around his waist while looking up at him. She stood on her tiptoes and kissed him. "I love you," she told him and laid her head against his chest. He sighed and hugged her too, kissing her forehead as he said, "I love you too."

She hugged him tighter and said softly, "Don't leave me."

He sighed as he told her, "I don't have a choice."

With her head against his chest, she asked, "Do you like that white girl?"

"Move Casey!" he said, trying to pull away from her but she held him tighter, not wanting to let him go. They stood there in silence for a moment and then Roman said, "Hey. I gotta go," gently pulling her arms from around his waist and caressing her face. He kissed her, and she opened her mouth and slid her tongue in his mouth and slowly kissed him. He took it and gently pulled, released and searched for it again. When they finally broke their kiss Casey's eyes were still closed as she slid her tongue over her bottom lip. He smiled when she opened her eyes and they were like slits of ecstasy.

"I'll call you," he told her and kissed her on the forehead. She nodded her head slowly, okay biting her bottom lip and went back in the house. When she closed the door, he thought about how hard this was because he didn't want to go, but he didn't have a choice. He also thought *Would their relationship last?* as he walked off.

CHAPTER VII

"Hey mama," he said when she walked in the kitchen.

"Good morning," Faye told him with a sleepy smile.

"Where's Isha?" she asked as she grabbed the teakettle and filled it with water.

"At Pecanland Mall," he answered while finishing his cereal as she put the kettle on the stove and turned it on.

"With who and what time is it?" she asked with a slight frown wondering how late she had slept.

"Well, judging by the clock on the wall.. It's 10:30am," he told her, nodding his head toward it.

She narrowed her eyes and thought, *I oughta pop him!*

"And she went with Aunt Kay," he added and got up and washed his bowl and spoon, knowing she didn't like them to leave dishes in the sink. He grinned as he thought about what she would always tell them.

"That brings roaches and you don't know who may come by." "Well!" Faye said, bringing him out of his thoughts.

"What Mama?" he asked, confused.

She shook her head as she looked at him and said, "you didn't hear a word I said, did you? That's a shame! I don't know what's wrong with you kids today! It's like your mind is a hundred miles away," then asked him seriously, "Are you doing that dope?"

"What? No!" he exclaimed and started laughing. "Where did that come from?" he asked, still laughing, knowing she was serious. *Mama out of control!* He thought.

"It's not funny either!" she said, glaring at him.

"I know. My bad" he said, holding his hands up and trying not to laugh.

"Anyway," she said, waving him off dismissively then told him, "What I asked you earlier was: do you have any plans for today?" "Oh, nothing. I plan on going to Skatetown tomorrow though," he told her then asked her, "Why?" leaning against the counter. "Because Frank and I are going out tonight and I want to know where you and Isha will be tonight," she told him as she put sugar and coffee in her coffee cup.

Roman frowned, but before he could say a word, she held up her hand and told him, "Hush. You and Isha are my children and I don't care how old y'all get y'all will always be my children. Now put some water in my cup and stir it while I make my toast," and smirked as the kettle started whistling.

"I love you too," he mumbled but did what she told him to do. She smiled to herself as she thought about how much she loved him and how much she would miss him when he left, but she knew it was for the best.

~

Someone fumbled with the phone as they picked it up.
A sleepy voice said, "Hello?"
It was hard to hear, so she said, "Hello?"
The groggy voice said, "Yeah."
"Is Roman there?" she asked.
"Yeah," the voice repeated.
"May I speak to him, please?" she asked.
"This is him," he said clearer.
"Oh," she said giggling and asked, "Did I wake you?"

"Naw. I always sound like this," he answered smartly. "Who am I speaking with?" he quipped.

"Jennifer," she told him.

He paused and asked, "Oh, what's up?" as he rolled on his side and looked at the clock which read 9:45pm.

"That's why I called you. I'm trying to find out," she told him.

"Is that right?" he asked chuckling then told her, "Look, I know you're probably with somebody and you know I'm with somebody, so what are you doing?"

"Do I have to spell it out?" she asked.

He laughed and said, "Naw, you don't but I do want you to get to the point. I mean, just be honest 'cause I know you're into me and I'm kind of into you."

"Kind of!" she said, offended.

"That's what I said," he told her coolly then said, "Jennifer, I don't know you and you don't know me. Yeah, I know of you just like you just know of me. I don't even know your last name, but what I do know is: my cousin Farrah probably gave you some information about me like me going to California soon and what happened to bring that about and probably told you my relationship with my girl probably wouldn't last. Am I on point?" he asked, knowing he was by her silence.

She took a deep breath and said, "Roman, listen. I do like you and I do want to get to know you, and yes, I know about you leaving soon and possibly never coming back, but I believe you will come back be it for summer vacation, the holidays, or whatever and I want to lay a foundation down with you now. I want to write to you and call you while you're there. If you don't mind, and I don't know anything about your relationship and neither do I care! She's the competition, so why would I care, and as far as me having a boyfriend: no I don't and in fact I'm giving that slot to you if you want it? So as you say 'what's up?'"

"You," he told her and asked, "When are you going back to school?" "Tomorrow," she said.

"Call me before you leave and always know that things come to you easier when you say what you mean and mean what you say."

"Okay, I will. Bye," she told him.

"Hello?" Faye answered the phone, laughing, trying to get away from Frank who was tickling her and trying to get her in the mood. "Hi. May I speak to Roman?" a female asked.

"Stop!" she said laughing and swatting Frank's hand away as she said, "He's not here right now. May I ask who's calling?"

"Okay. Would you tell him that Jennifer called please?" she answered.

"Jennifer? Farrah's friend Jennifer?" she asked as she held up her index finger signaling Frank to stop. Play time was over!

"Yes ma'am. How are you doing," Jennifer responded.

"I'm fine," Faye said as she sat on her bed and crossed her legs. "Jennifer, why are you calling Roman?" she asked her bluntly. Caught off guard, she answered, "We went to the game together Friday and he asked me to call him before I went back to school," watching her tone and being respectful but also wondering if there was a problem.

"Oh. Well he's not here, but I'll tell him you called," Faye told her, not feeling her calling her son.

"Thank you. Bye," Jennifer responded and hung up.

Faye looked at Frank as she hung up the phone.

"What?" he asked, looking at her and wanting to get back to what they had going on!

"That was Jennifer," she said.

"And?" he asked, not getting the point.

"Farrah's white friend Jennifer," she told him.

"Faye!" he said sharply.

She put her hands up saying, "I know! I know, Frank and I'm not prejudiced, but there are people in this city who are prejudiced, and I don't want him getting caught up in that mess!" She hoped he would understand.

He shook his head and told her, "Faye, there's not a day that goes by that you don't think of some reason to worry about Roman! He's okay, so let him live and, if he wants to date a white girl, let him! He's going to California, anyway!"

She shrugged her shoulders, sighing as Frank squeezed her hand and said, "Now, how about some hot mix?" as he smiled and grabbed her waist.

"Let me go, Frank!" she told him trying to get away, but it was too late! He wrapped his arms around her and laid her on their bed. She was laughing and still trying to get away, but when his kisses brushed her neck and found her lips, she surrendered and they engaged in some "hot mix."

~

"Roman! Why haven't you put your skates on?"

"I'm not ready," he told her.

"Well, why did you come?" she asked, getting frustrated.

"Because I wanted to be with you," he told her.

"Good answer," she said smiling. He took his skates off his shoulder and began to put them on.

Casey looked at him and said sarcastically, "Oh, now you wanna put them on!"

"Yep! Let's go," he said, grabbing her hand and heading toward the floor. Skatedown on 165 North was packed. It always was on Sundays. The projection screen was playing the video of the song they were skating too. People were skating while some couples were making out in the corners. Roman and Casey skated together on most songs and alone on some like when it was "ladies" or "fellas" only. A fight broke out and security came and broke it up with the quickness! Of course, it was females! That's who it was most of the time! As the night went on he and Casey skated until the deejay announced it was the last song and the lights came on. People started heading toward the door to catch their rides and get to their cars before the traffic jam. He and Casey stayed back to miss the crowd and to give their ride time to make it here to pick them up. When the crowd got smaller, they went outside to wait. Onika drove up, and they both got in the backseat.

"What's up?" he asked as Casey said, "Hey girl."

"Hey?" she said to both of them as the interior light came on and went off when they closed the door. There was a line of cars, but after a while they made it out of the parking lot. They all talked as they rode home. Roman was talking to Onika as he slid his hand under Casey's skirt. He eased her panties to the side and slipped his finger inside her and began moving it in her wetness. She couldn't get over how bold he was but knew that he would try to get away with something without getting caught. *His name fit: Chance*, she thought as he played with her spot. His jacket stayed over her lap as he kept fingering her and talking to Onika. He started using his index finger and curved it up inside of her and wiggled it. When he did, she moaned and slightly moved her hips. He had found her spot. She started moaning more, and he whispered, "shh" as he kept talking to Onika. Casey kept rolling on his finger as they passed Renwick Street and were coming to a red light. It turned green, and they kept going as he kept fingering her and talking to Onika. Casey got close as they neared the exit to their neighborhood. As they waited on the light to turn green Casey started to cum and he felt it shoot all over his finger and he kept working it. He got hard when she came because he hadn't ever fingered her to an orgasm before. He looked at her and her eyes were closed with her mouth parted and her breathing labored. She grabbed his neck, pulled him toward her and slid her tongue into his mouth, kissing him passionately! When they made it to his house, Onika pulled in his driveway and cleared her throat saying, "ahem. We're here." They broke their kiss.

"Thanks for the ride, Onika," he said.

"You're welcome" she told him.

He looked at Casey and told her, "I'll see you tomorrow, baby."

"Okay. Bye," she told him and laid back against the seat. When they drove off, he looked at his hand.

~

Spring Carnival! It was a beautiful day with the sun shining and clear skies! It was the perfect day for the carnival and also a day when everybody ditched class because there wasn't any class, only homeroom! There were booths everywhere! Dunking booths, kissing booths, booths for throwing water balloons, booths to shoot basketball, and many others. There were concession stands selling cheeseburgers, hotdogs, tamales, cotton candy, fountain drinks, and other foods. Students were taking pictures, getting yearbooks signed, and enjoying themselves. There were also chicks walking around with tight shorts, skimpy skirts, and even some of the teachers had some on and looked good Roman thought as he walked around with Trey, Gerald, and Cotton. He had on a pair of white oversized Nike shorts, a matching button down Nike shirt with a wife-beater under it, and a pair of canvas style Nike shoes with Nike socks. He also had on a Turkish rope and a pair of tinted wide frame Ray-Bans with his hair combed back in a sea of shining black curls. They were chilling and enjoying this day! They were also trying to find a place where they could go smoke some of the weed they bought last night as he laughed, listening to Trey bag on Cotton and they were going at it too!

"You a lie chump! You don't know what I do!" Cotton said.

"Yeah right! Everybody knows you love to eat coochie!" Trey told him, not believing him. Roman and Gerald were rolling!

"Say! Ain't nothin' wrong wit' it, homie! If you eat it, you just eat it!" Gerald told him laughing. Roman and Trey laughed too.

Cotton frowned! "Say! I done told y'all I don't eat! I don't get down like that!" he said, trying to convince them!

"That's not what we heard, playa," Roman told him, shaking his head.

"Yeah! Gobble! Gobble!" Trey said quickly and they all burst out laughing, even Cotton. Roman was drinking some soda and almost choked as Trey imitated a turkey and oral sex!

Roman had tears in his eyes and pulled his shades off to wipe his eyes as he said, "Stop! Please stop!"

"For what?" Trey asked.

"He knows it's true! Don't chu?" he said, looking at Cotton quickly and bucking his eyes!

"Y'all trippin'! I don't eat!" Cotton told them again!

Gerald said, "Leave him alone, Trey!"

"All right, all right!" he said, nodding his head and holding up his hands.

"But chu know it's true, right!" he told him, turning his head quickly to look at him!

They all laughed and Roman said, "Shut up Trey! Let's go!" as they walked, and he kept bagging on him.

There are just some things you don't tell! Cotton thought as he kept lying.

~

"Commencement starts at 7 o'clock," Faye told him as they walked through the supermarket trying to get some last minute items for Isha's small graduation party before they went to pick up her cake. Roman was pushing the cart as they went down the aisle.

"I don't know why you're having her party before the graduation," he told her as he ate a Jolly Rancher, his favorite candy.

She told him, "Well, I know there's gonna be a lot of parties after the graduation, so I'd rather have it before so she can go enjoy

94

herself afterwards," as she picked up some chips and put them in the cart.

Roman looked at her and said, "Yeah right!" as he burst out laughing.

"What?" Faye asked smiling.

"You know what. You just don't wanna deal with a lot of people and clean up after them," he told her laughing.

She laughed knowing it was true and said, "don't tell anybody." "You got it," he told her as they laughed and continued shopping. When they were going down another aisle, Faye asked, "So, are you ready to leave?" watching him closely.

He sighed and answered her, "No!" truthfully.

"Well, I already got your ticket, Roman!" she told him matter-of-factly.

He looked at her and, sounding ungrateful, said, "I know. A bus ticket."

She got defensive and said, "Roman, that was all I could do with everything going on and Isha's graduation and your dad is having a hard time right now and I hope things turn around for him and Jewel, especially after he helped me with Isha's graduation gift, then lost his job and had to move out of his house on East 48th Street and into an apartment in Watts! But at least he got another job working with your Uncle Ron!"

He felt bad and just said, "I know. It's cool," not really liking taking the bus, especially since he didn't really want to go in the first place. When they came out of the store, Roman put the bags in the trunk and they went to get Isha's cake. She did not know her mother was going to do this and was surprised! Her mom, Frank, Roman, Grandma Francine, Aunt Kay, Aunt Jasmine, Casey and Onika gathered around the table telling her to cut the cake! Isha was having a great time as she got gifts, cash, and was on speakerphone with her dad, his girlfriend Jewel, and her half brother and sister. She was laughing when her dad asked, "Have you gotten your surprise yet?"

"Not yet!" Faye said quickly and loud enough for him to hear her. Isha and Roman looked at their mom curiously but Faye ignored them both trying to play it off!

"Oh! Well let me know when you do," Paul said laughing.

"I will," Isha answered confused because she thought she had gotten all her gifts. When it got close to 5:30pm, the party ended and Isha had to be at the Monroe Civic Center at 6 o'clock so she went into her room and grabbed her cap and gown. She said her goodbyes and her Aunt Kay drove her to the Civic Center. Everybody else helped Faye clean up and then they all got into their cars and headed to the graduation except Frank. He stayed at the house. They made it to the Civic Center early and found seats without a problem. Frank showed up and sat beside Faye at 6:50pm. He was there earlier, but it took him a while to find her because it was so crowded. She whispered something in his ear and he nodded yes. After the speeches, the commencement went quickly and when Isha's name was called her family and friends cheered! Drake, Farrah, and other members of her family on her mom and dad's side were clapping and whistling as she walked across the stage smiling and dancing causing people to laugh. When the principal presented the graduating class, they pushed the tassels on their caps to the opposite side and threw their caps in the air cheering loudly! Later, everybody was taking pictures with their kids, relatives and friends and congratulating them on graduating!

Isha was still taking pictures outside when Faye asked, "Where is Frank? I need more film." looking around for him.

"I don't know," Grandma Francine answered, looking around too. "He was here a minute ago," Casey told her, wondering where Roman was too.

"Mama, I'm ready to go and you're out of film!" Isha told her ready to go hang out with her friends and celebrate!

"Where is Frank and Roman?!" Faye asked, sounding like she was getting pissed! She looked at her sister and asked, "Kay, you and Jasmine rode together?"

"Yeah," Kay answered then Faye looked at her mama and asked, "Mama you drove your car didn't you?"

"Yeah baby I drove mine," Grandma Francine told her.

Roman is riding with Casey and Onika she said to herself and looked at Isha and asked her, "Who are you riding with?"

"Huh?" Isha responded in confusion.

"I said..who are you riding with?" she repeated slowly.

"Probably with herself," somebody said as a car stopped in front of all of them. It was Roman and Frank in a brand new Mustang convertible! Isha started screaming and jumping up and down! "Mama! Whose car is this? Is this my car?" she said excitedly, running up to her mom and grabbing her arm hoping this is her car!"

"No!" Faye said playfully and then said, "Yeah baby, it's yours!" smiling.

Isha started screaming and jumping up again! "Oh, my God! I can't believe this! Mama when!" she exclaimed as tears fell from her eyes! People looked and wondered what was going on as Grandma Francine and Aunt Kay looked on crying too.

"That's tight!" Casey said as she admired the car. It was a money green convertible Mustang with a white top and factory chrome rims.

"Wow!" Onika said, liking the car.

"Isha," Faye started to say as she lifted her daughter's chin and tried to wipe away her tears, but they kept coming. "This is the surprise your dad was hinting about," she continued. "Frank, Paul, Jewel, and I are proud of you and we bought this car for you, so, when you go to college, you won't have any trouble coming home or going back to school."

She and Frank hugged Isha as she kept crying and told them, "thank you."

"You're welcome!" he told her, smiling with his wife.

"Yeah, yeah, yeah. Let's go," Roman said, interrupting them.

"Shut up, Roman!" Casey said and everybody laughed.

"What?" he asked like nothing was wrong and said, "I'm happy for her and I know she's happy! Look at her! So let's go! I know I would be ready to go if this was my car so I know she's ready! I'd be ready to leave all of y'all!" he told them, laughing.

Isha started laughing and told him, "Hush chump!" as she hugged him with tears in her eyes.

"Here you go," Frank said, handing her the keys and told her, "Be careful and don't stay out too late."

"I will and I won't," she told him and got in her car. She started it up and told everyone "bye," as she drove off.

"I'm so proud of her," Grandma Francine said aloud.

"Me too, Mama," Faye said looking at her mama. They all said their goodbyes and went their separate ways. As he and Faye drove home, Frank wondered when he and Faye would start trying to have kids.

~

"Hi Roman," Casey's mom said as she opened the door for him. "Hi, how are you doing?" he asked as she closed the door.

"I'm fine," she told him walking into the den and said, "So, I hear you're leaving soon," as she sat down.

"Yes, ma'am. In fact, I'm leaving tomorrow," he told her, sitting down to talk to her for a minute. He liked her and looked at her like a second mom. She was always nice to him and showed him kindness even when he got in trouble.

"Oh, well, are you looking forward to it?" she asked.

"Not really because I don't want to go but what can I do?" he answered truthfully.

She said, "hmm. Well, I know Faye wouldn't do this if she didn't feel like this was the right thing to do, son."

He didn't agree but out of respect told her, "Yes, ma'am. You're probably right," then asked, "Is Casey in her room?" to change the subject.

"No, she's in the back. You can go back there," she told him.

"Okay. See you later," he told her.

"See you later baby," she told him as he went toward the back.

The back wasn't a room but a guest apartment. It was fully furnished with a sleeper sofa, a couch, chairs, refrigerator, stove, a fully stocked bar, barstools, carpeted, air-conditioned, and a bathroom with a shower. It was a place where family and friends came to watch movies, football games, basketball games, boxing, hanging out or just to sleep. He opened the door and Casey was lying on the sofa bed with a two-piece *Yosemite Sam* pajamas while watching a movie.

She looked up and smiled as she said, "Hey. What are you doing here?"

"Coming to see you," he told her, smiling. "I see you're just lounging," he told her as she moved over so he could sit on the bed. "You haven't answered my question," she said playfully. "What are you doing here?" she asked again, rubbing her legs against him.

He looked at her and rubbed her hips as he told her, "I came by to let you know I'm leaving tomorrow."

She sighed and looked up at the ceiling.

"Did you hear me?" he asked her knowing she did.

"Yeah, I heard you," she mumbled, still looking at the ceiling. "And?" he said.

"And what, Roman! You're leaving! What do you want me to say!" she snapped. Her voice cracked, and she began to cry.

"Come here," he said softly as he pulled her closer to him and into his lap.

"You're leaving me," she said through tears.

He held her tighter and told her, "I'm sorry. You know I don't want to but I have to, baby. We can call and write to each other though" as he wiped away her tears.

She frowned and said angrily, "tsk! I don't wanna write! I wanna see you! Everyday!"

He took a deep breath and asked, "So what are you gonna do, Casey? Are you gonna stay down with me or lay it down?"

Silence.

"I don't know, Roman," she finally told him, averting her eyes and then looked at him and repeated, "I don't know."

He kissed her on her lips and forehead, told her, "I'm out" and got up to leave because, even if she didn't say it, her eyes said it all! She watched him as he walked to the door, and, when he opened it she told him, "Roman! I love you!" her voice cracking.

He looked at her and told her, "I love you too, Casey! Stay sweet." then closed the door behind him. She was hurting and, as tears rolled down her face, she laid down and sobbed loudly.

~

"Are you ready?" she asked when she came into his room.

He looked up and told her, "Yes, ma'am. I'm ready" as he locked the latch on his luggage.

"Where's Isha?" Faye asked as she walked out in the hallway and looked down the hall toward her room.

"She and Frank burned off," he told her.

"What?" she said, confused by what he said.

He chuckled and said, "They left, mama, and we already said our goodbyes. They asked if I wanted them to go with us, but I told them no, so they went to look for a car cover for Isha's car."

"Okay. Well, your food is ready and I have your money," she told him as he started taking his luggage to the car.

"That was the last one," he told her when he came back into the house.

"I'm gonna miss you," she said as she sat in the living room crying quietly.

He walked over and hugged his mom as he said, "I'm gonna miss you too, Mama, but don't cry. Let's go." They drove downtown to the bus station and when they made it there, they made sure his ticket was in order, checked his luggage, and made sure the bus would arrive on time. The schedule showed the bus would arrive in fifteen minutes and would leave ten minutes afterward, so they sat and talked.

"Be careful, son," she told him.

"I will, Mama. I'm good," he told her again, laughing. The bus arrived, and he told her, "this is it," when they started calling for passengers to board the bus.

"Yeah, I guess it is," she told him as she stood up with him. She was crying.

He shook his head. "Mama, you gotta stop crying. Call dad and let him know I'm on my way and I'll call you when I make it there in three days," he told her.

"Okay," she said, still crying. He couldn't stand seeing her cry, but neither could he understand why she was crying because it was her idea to send him to California. He pulled away from her, picked up his duffel bag, and placed it on his shoulder. She waved goodbye when he got to the bus. The driver checked his ticket, he got on the bus, found a window seat, and got comfortable.

Faye drove home crying and saying, "What have I done? Have I lost my son?" but it was like Roman said, "what's done is done, so California here he comes!"

Roman wished he could have slept the whole way through Texas. There were so many stops: it was ridiculous and going through West Monroe, Ruston, Grambling, Shreveport, and other parts of Louisiana was nothing compared to going through Texas. It was taking a day and a half or almost two days just to get out of Texas. These were his thoughts as he sat next to an older woman who reminded him of his dad's girlfriend's mom. He laughed as he thought about some episodes he got himself into as a kid in California. Especially the time he called Isha the "b" word at Jewel's mom's house! When he did, she grabbed his arm and took him into the bathroom.

He thought she was about to whip him but she said, "I'm not going to spank you!" and he smiled until she said, "But I am going to do this!" turning the water on in the sink and showing him a bar of soap!"

Yep! She was going to wash his mouth out with soap! He tried to get away, but she kept her grip on his arm as she ran water over the soap!

"Open your mouth!" she told him but Roman shook his head trying to get away from her. He saw Isha watching out of the corner of his eye and wanted to go smack her as she laughed.

"Snitch!" he mumbled! She grabbed his nose and caused him to open his mouth and put the soap in his mouth! Roman was mad and the taste of the soap made him angrier and it was all on his teeth! When it was over, she told him to "rinse his mouth." He did and went into a room and didn't say a word until his dad came to pick them up! He wished his mom was here but knew that he would've gotten worse if she was because she didn't play when it came to him calling his sister names, especially curse names! But the truth is when Jewel's mom washed his mouth out with soap it worked because he never cursed around her again! He started thinking about some of the good times he had in California like when his dad took them to Disneyland, the prehistoric museum, zoos, camping in Santa Barbara, parks, and restaurants. He remembered the time when he, Jewel, his dad, and Isha went to a Spanish restaurant and met the martial artist and actor Jim Kelly. His dad told him to go and ask him for his autograph and he did and when Isha saw him come back with an autograph, then she went over there and got one too. He kept looking toward the man's table and when the man picked up a bowl of super hot sauce and drank the whole thing he and Isha said, "dang" in unison gawking at him! Jewel told them to stop it while their dad just laughed at them. Roman settled in his seat and thought about when he was younger and his dad was with a white woman named Sharon. His birthday was the next day and he couldn't sleep because he knew he had a birthday cake in the refrigerator and he wanted that cake! His dad and Sharon were asleep, so he snuck out of bed, went into the kitchen, opened the refrigerator, and there was his cake! He looked to see if anybody was coming, then looked back at his cake, took his little hand and grabbed as much cake as he could and started eating it. He was dropping crumbs everywhere and not even realizing it. He closed the refrigerator door back and tried to wipe the evidence off of his hand. He went back to his room and went back to sleep.

The next morning he heard Sharon say, "Paul, come and look at this." He shut his eyes tight pretending to be asleep then heard his dad call him.

"Roman," Paul said, but he wouldn't answer.

"I know you're not asleep," Paul said.

"Huh?" Roman mumbled pretending to be asleep, but Paul wasn't fooled.

"Get up and you know what. Come on," he told him and Roman followed him to the dining room. Sharon had the cake on the table with the candles lit. She giggled when she saw him and said, "Happy birthday, Roman." He smiled and said, "Happy birthday to me." His dad put him in a chair and said, "make a wish and blow out the candles because you already had the first piece of cake," and started laughing. Sharon laughed too. Roman looked at the handprint on the cake and blew out the candles! Later that day his dad and Sharon took him to Tijuana and bought him a sombrero, a vest and some maracas. His dad also had another girlfriend named

Cindy. Roman always wondered why every time he walked in the bedroom she was naked and her boobs and her butt were always lighter than the rest of her body. Then there was Gina. Gina was very beautiful and Roman meant beautiful. She and his dad took him and his sister Isha to Hollywood Park in Inglewood to the racetrack and they would choose horses and then place bets on them and they won quite a lot. On the other hand, when they went to Griffith Park Roman would lose a lot. He and Isha would ride horses around the track at Griffith Park. They would get strapped into these saddle seats on the horses and no matter what Isha always seemed to beat Roman and he hated it. His dad and Gina would laugh but he didn't think it was funny because not only was he losing to a girl but he was losing to his sister. Anyway, Gina faded out and when Roman and Isha came back Jewel was his dad's girlfriend. She, her sister Mona, their Uncle Brad, Isha, and he had a lot of fun together. They went swimming, to amusement parks, camping, and also had water fights in the house. They also had fun on the city buses because his dad drove buses for RTD which is the city bus system for Los Angeles and on his dad's breaks he would call Jewel and tell her to meet him somewhere then she'd meet him, park the car and they would get on the bus and ride across the city. It was cool with just the four of them on that big bus. They also went to a lot of movies and beaches like Redondo, Venice, Santa Monica, and Marina del Rey. They went to Marineland a lot too. His dad had a little red MG Midget and Roman was sitting there comfortably in his seat wondering if he still had it. Yeah, he was missing California. The bus passed through Mexico and Arizona and was now crossing the California border! "Bout time!" he said to himself when he saw the *Welcome to California* sign because when the bus was about to cross the Mexico border he had to hide his fruit and food because officers came on the bus to make sure nobody had these or other perishable items because of fruit flies but he was not about to come out of his pocket for anything! The bus finally pulled into the Greyhound and

Amtrak station! It was 1:15pm, and he wondered if his dad would pick him up but then figured that he and Jewel were still at work and the kids were probably at school and daycare. When he got off the bus and walked to the terminal, he saw murals and signs everywhere of the Olympics that had recently been here. He was looking around for Paul and waiting on the people to unload the luggage off the bus. He was ready to get home because he needed a bath and a haircut! Thirty minutes later he finally got his luggage, but there was still no sign of Paul.

"There he is!" he heard somebody yell, followed by, "Roman! Over here!"

He looked and saw his Uncle Ron and his cousin Noah waving at him! He was glad to see them! He couldn't believe he didn't see his Uncle sooner because he's every bit of 6' 10 and 380 pounds! He was a former football player for the NFL before he messed up his knee 3 years after he married his Aunt Barabara. Funny thing is his Aunt Barbara is only 5 2' so Roman never understood how they were a good match but to each his own.

When they made it to him, Noah asked him, "What's up? Have you been here long?" as he hugged him and his Uncle Ron slapped him on his shoulder and also asked, "What's up, boy? Are you ready to go?" as people looked at him but what would you expect because at 6' 10 and how his voice carried, he commanded attention!

Roman said, "Yes sir. I'm ready," then asked him, "Where's Dad?" "Oh, he and Jewel are at work, so you're going over to our house until your dad gets off," he told him as he and Noah helped him carry his luggage. When they made it to his Uncle's car and got the luggage inside, they asked him if he was hungry and he told them, "Naw, I already ate." They turned and looked at him.

He laughed and said, "Mama put some food together for me for the trip."

"Oh," his Uncle said, and they shook their heads in understanding. "So, where are you going to school?" Noah asked.

"I don't know. What district am I in?" Roman asked him.

"Well, Uncle Paul lives in Watts, and the closest school is Centennial so you'll probably go there," Noah told him.

"Okay. What school do you go to?" he asked Noah.

"I attend Fairfax." he answered.

"Oh. Where do y'all live?" Roman asked him.

Noah laughed and said, "y'all! No homie! You've got to lose that accent!"

"We live in your dad's old house on East 48th," his uncle answered, glancing at him in the rearview mirror.

"What?" Roman said, confused.

"Yeah. I thought you knew. When your dad moved, we moved into the house because we needed a bigger place and since your Uncle Lawrence owns it, he agreed," his uncle told him.

"What about Mr. and Mrs. Riffin? Do they still live next door?" he asked.

"No. Mr. Riffin died a year and a half ago and his wife sold the house and moved to Milwaukee to live with her daughter," his uncle told him.

"You serious?" Roman asked, stunned.

"Yes. I thought you knew." Noah answered.

"Naw, I didn't know," Roman stammered.

"Brenda and her daughter Lisa live there now. You'll meet them," Noah told him.

"Alright," Roman said.

As they rode to the house his uncle asked him if he wanted to work with him on weekends, holidays and his school breaks to keep money in his pocket and to help him buy clothes and tennis shoes when he needed them. He told him he'd think about it. When they made it to East 48th Street a rush of memories came to him about the Riffins. They were a nice elderly black couple that he and

Isha would always spend time with like when their dad and Jewel needed a babysitter or when they just wanted to get out of the house. There were times when they would be in their backyard playing and Mr. Riffin would come outside and ask him if he could have some lemons because they had apricot and lemon trees in their backyard and he would say, "Yes sir," and run into the house and ask his dad for a basket and he'd ask him why he needed one and he would tell him because Mr. Riffin wants some lemons and he had to get him some and his dad would laugh and give him a basket. He also remembered how Mr. Riffin's wife would cook for him and Isha and how much Mrs. Riffin liked them too. He wondered if Isha knew everything Uncle Ron had told him about the Riffins.

When they pulled into the driveway, he looked at the house and it looked the same, starting from the huge porch, freshly cut lawn and beautiful flowers.

As they were taking his luggage out of the car, he heard his cousin Rikki say, "Barbara, Roman's here!"

He laughed because she was loud just like her dad and looked just like him. Rikki is Uncle Ron's biological daughter and Noah is his adopted son. His Aunt Barbara had Noah before she met Rikki's dad Uncle Ron but he looked at him as his own. He looked at Rikki as she stood on the porch smiling.

"Barbara!" she yelled again, calling for his aunt. Roman could never understand how Rikki could get away with calling her mom by her first name and not mama. He hugged her as they sat his luggage down in the living room.

"Hey boyy!" he heard his aunt say and smiled when he turned around and saw her face! She was smiling too! "Come and give your aunt a hug," she said as she stretched out her arms toward him. He hugged her as he looked at her pretty black skin. His family called her *Black* because she was just that: *Black* and Beautiful.

"Let me look at you," she said as she pulled away and turned him around. He hated this part!

"Still growing and looking just like your Daddy," she said smiling at him.

"Yes, ma'am," he said embarrassed.

"He's polite!" Rikki said and laughed.

"I know! I told him that he has to get rid of that accent too!" Noah said laughing.

"Leave him alone! That's home training! You and Rikki need to learn it!" his aunt chided them.

"Yeah, right!" Noah said while at the same time Rikki said "O-kay!" which meant "be for real!" or "you gotta be kidding!" They laughed and caught up on old times and then there were nothing but questions and answers. They asked the questions, and he gave the answers, but he was tired and ready to go home and relax! *Maybe soon* he thought.

CHAPTER VIII

It was the first day of Carrollette and Band Camp and also the third day that Roman had been gone and Casey had been stressed all day and really wasn't feeling practice. She missed him and it was driving her crazy but thought *Why can't I deal with a long-distance relationship? He did promise me it would work* as she waited on her mom to come pick her up so she could go home, take a bath and relax.

"What's up, C?" somebody asked her from behind.

She turned to see who it was and said, "Hey, Craig. What's up?"

He walked closer to her and said, "Nothing, just thinking about you."

She sighed and said, "yeah right" while rolling her eyes. "You know that Roman's gone, don't you?" she asked looking right at him.

He was surprised that she could read him like that and tried to hide it as he said, "Well, yeah: I heard he was gone but I want to know what's up with you. Is that a problem?" he asked, looking in her eyes.

She sighed and said, "Craig, I don't know. It's too soon."

He frowned and asked, "What do you mean?"

"What I mean is: Roman just left and I still love him and I'm not sure if I want to be with anybody else," she told him.

He was agitated. He said, "Well, look: he's not here, and I bet he's not in California thinking or worrying about you or what you're doing here."

She tilted her head to the side and snapped: "You don't know what he's thinking about or doing there!" getting angry now.

He saw that he had mis-stepped and tried to clean it up by saying, "Whoa! What I mean is, I hear that he's not coming back, so why sweat it?"

She frowned at him and said, "look!" but he held up his hands and cut her off by saying, "wait a minute! I'm not sweatin' you or talkin' 'bout him: I'm just talkin' about me and you." He pulled a pen and piece of paper out, started writing and asked, "Whenever you get some free time call me because I really want to get to know you. Cool?" he asked and held the paper out to her as she just looked at him but finally took it. He smiled and said again, "call me," just as her mom drove up. Stacy was watching them from inside the lobby. She smiled and came out when she saw her mom drive up too.

"Hey Craig," she said, smiling as she passed them and gave him a thumbs up and a wink discreetly as she got into the car. She had set the entire thing up because Casey would forget about Roman one way or another.

~

"So what are you going to do when you get home?" Noah asked Roman as they sat and talked in his old room which was now Noah's room looking at some magazines.

"Unpack, take a bath, and go to sleep" he responded looking through the magazine, then asked, "What else you got in that wall?" referring to the hiding spot where Noah got the porno magazines.

"Do you get high?" Noah asked straight out, looking at him and waiting for an answer.

"Fo'sho! Why?" Roman asked.

"This!" Noah said as he reached in the wall and pulled out a shoe box and when he opened it, there were some rolling papers, weed and a lighter in it.

"Bet!" Roman said as he grabbed the sack, opened it, and inhaled the weed.

"What kind is it?" he asked, looking at Noah.

"Indo" Noah responded.

Roman said, "I ain't never had that."

"You will," Noah said matter-of-factly. He chuckled and said, "But you have got to get rid of that accent, cousin! For real!" he added, laughing.

"Yeah, aight!" Roman said frowning, then added, "I don't see what's so funny!" getting agitated.

"Your accent, cousin!" Noah answered laughing.

"Put this stuff back up!" Roman told him to change the subject. They kept kicking it and talking about hanging out this weekend. Roman's first thought was he had to get him some clothes. As they talked, the doorbell rang.

"That's probably your dad," Noah said looking at him.

"You're probably right," he responded as they got up, walked out the room, and headed toward the living room.

"Barbara! Uncle Paul is hereee!" Rikki shouted.

"Yeah, your Dad's here!" Noah said as he looked at Roman and burst out laughing. Rikki's a trip, just like her dad. They walked into the living room and saw Paul hugging Rikki and she was loving it. She always liked attention. Barbara walked out of her bedroom and closed the door because Ron was taking a nap.

"Hey bro," she said when she came into the living room.

"Hey Black," he said smiling at her and asked, "What have you been up to?" walking over to her and hugging her.

"Trying to keep this money straight," she said as they broke their embrace then added, "You know how Ron is when it comes to money! Spend, spend, spend and never think about a budget," shaking her head at the thought. He understood but didn't say anything because that was something they needed to work out for themselves and it was not his business.

"Where's Man?" he asked, changing the subject.

"Right here," Roman said, walking into the living room with Noah. Paul smiled. He was glad to see his son.

"What's up, Pop?" he said smiling as he walked over to his dad to show him some love.

"Pop!" he said, frowning and poking him in his side.

Roman laughed and said, "my bad!" trying to block him.

"So how was your trip?" he asked after letting him go.

"Long," Roman replied, sighing.

"What's up Noah?" Paul asked his nephew.

"Chilling. Where's Amie and Bryan?" he asked.

"They're probably home with Jewel by now," he answered and looked at Roman and asked, "Are you ready to go? I know you're tired."

"Yeah, I am on both counts," he replied, then asked, "But when can I come back?"

"Soon," he replied.

"Cool," he said and looked at Noah.

"Is this all your luggage?" Paul asked, looking at the suitcases in the living room.

"Yeah, that's it," Roman answered.

"Well, let's go" Paul said and hugged his sister and niece and told them he would see them later and Roman did the same. He, Paul, and Noah took his luggage outside and put it in Paul's truck Roman was surprised when he saw the truck but said nothing. It was old, and it was a white Ford full-size truck with peeling paint. They got in and drove off and made a right on McKinley and a left on 48th Place, then made a right on Central going toward Watts.

"Have you called your mom yet?" Paul asked as he drove.

"Not yet. I was waiting till I got home so I wouldn't charge Aunt Barbara's phone bill," he answered.

"All right," Paul said nodding his head then added, "But you need to call her before you do anything else 'cuz I don't want her to worry and knowing her she's sitting by the phone right now," he said and started laughing.

Roman laughed too, knowing he was probably right. They talked about the move and the reasons why and he told him about how Isha acted when she got into her car. They made it to 92nd and made a left. They made a right on Success and pulled into a big driveway where there were four cars. Roman was confused but then understood when they parked behind his dad's Camaro. There were two apartments in the front and two behind them. It was like a complex within a chain-link fence with four mini-houses.

Jewel, Bryan, and Amie came out the door.

"Roman! Roman!" Amie and Bryan said excitedly and ran to the truck, happy to see their brother.

He smiled at them and said, "Hey! What's up?" happy to see them too. He hugged and kissed them both, then looked at them and laughed because Bryan looked like a miniature of their father and Amie looked like a miniature Prince. She even had hazel eyes like him. Paul looked on and laughed. They were ignoring him today. He grabbed some of Roman's luggage to take inside.

"Hi baby," he said to Jewel, kissing her before going inside.

"Hi," she said kissing him back then said, "I see that they're happy to see him!" laughing as she watched them smother him.

"Yeah," he said, glancing over his shoulder at them and going inside.

"Let me get my luggage," Roman told them, trying to get them inside. They were asking him a thousand questions and not thinking about going inside.

"Do you want me to help you?" Bryan asked him.

"Naw, I got it," he answered.

"I can help you too," Amie said, trying to imitate her brother.

"I got it, boo" Roman told her, smiling at his little sister.

"Hey Jewel," he said when he made it upstairs.

"Hi Man. I'm glad you're here," she told him and kissed him on his cheek.

"Thanks," he said as Amie chimed in, "me too! Me too!" They started laughing.

"Amie, let him go inside!" Bryan said, trying to move her out the way.

"Stop it!" she whined.

"Break it up you two and go in the house!" Paul told them, putting an end to their argument. "It's the second room on the left," Paul told him and went outside to get his last two suitcases. Roman walked into his room or *their room,* he thought as he looked around. There was a set of bunk beds and a twin-size bed in the room. *I guess that's mine,* he thought, looking at the twin bed.

"I know it's small but just hold on because we'll be moving soon," Paul told him, walking in and setting the other suitcases down.

"It's cool," Roman said looking around.

"Don't forget to call your mom. In fact, you can do it now," Paul told him.

"You can use the phone in my room," he added.

"Amie and Bryan! Come here!" he shouted.

"Okay!" they said in unison, running into the room. Jewel came in behind them.

"Good!" Paul said when he saw her there and said, "Baby, take Roman in our room and let him use the phone. Amie and Bryan started toward the door.

"No! Stay in here with me," Paul told him.

"Daddy!" Amie whined as Bryan said, "I want to go with Roman". "Do as I say!" Paul said. They got quiet and started pouting.

"It's on the nightstand, Roman" Jewel said, showing him the phone. "We'll be in the kitchen when you finish," she added and started to close the door.

"Thanks," he said.

"You're welcome," she said and closed the door.

"Hello?" Frank said answering the phone.

"What's up Frank?" Roman asked, glad that he answered the phone so he could surprise his mom.

"Roman? Is that you?" he asked, wanting to be sure before calling Faye.

"Yeah, it's me," he answered, smiling on the phone.

"Where are you? I'll get your mom," he said, about to call Faye. "Naw, wait!" he said quickly.

"Why?" he asked.

"I wanna surprise her," he said, then asked, "What has she been doing since I left?"

"Boo-hooing!" Frank said matter-of-factly, then added, "she's been driving me and Isha crazy worrying about you!"

Roman chuckled. "How's Isha?" he asked.

"She's good just enjoying her car and your space," he told him laughing.

"Huh?" Roman said in confusion.

"Your room!" he said. "Every time we look around, she's in there. I believe she just misses you," he told him seriously.

"Let me talk to her," he told him.

"All right. Hold on," he said.

"Isha!" he yelled, covering the phone with his hand.

"Huh?" Roman heard her say.

"Telephone!" Frank told her.

"I got it!" she said, picking up her phone.

115

"Hello?" she said after Frank hung up.

"What's up ugly?" he asked.

"Roman!" she screeched!

"Where are you?" she demanded, glad to hear from her brother.

"In L.A." he answered.

"Oh, and you the ugly one, chump!" she told him, giggling.

"Naw! That's your title!" he said.

"Shut up!" she told him and burst out laughing! They talked for a few more minutes and then she told him, "I'm so glad you called!" "Why?" he asked.

"Mama!" she responded. *"I wonder where he is. What have I done?"* she said, mimicking their mother.

They both burst out laughing!

"Isha, you are too loud in here!" Faye said, opening Isha's door. "Mama-" she started to say, but Roman cut her off and said, "tell her your friend said, 'mind her business'."

"What!" she said in surprise.

"Do it!" he said laughing.

She looked at her mother and said, "Mama, my friend said to mind your business" while trying to keep a straight face.

Faye looked shocked then snapped, "Give me that phone!," snatching it away from Isha!

"Look! I-" she said, but was cut off when Roman said, "Yeah, yeah, yeah! What's up, woman?"

Isha laughed as she saw her mother's expression change from anger, confusion, recognition, then to shock.

She couldn't stop laughing! If only she could've taken a picture! "Roman!" was all she could say!

"And only," he responded, laughing.

"Hey baby. Where are you?" she asked with tears in her eyes.

"I'm at Dad's. I made it here half an hour ago," he responded. "Mama," Isha said, getting up and going over to her and rubbing her back when she noticed her crying.

"I'm all right. I'm just glad to hear from him," she said, wiping away her tears.

"When did you call? I didn't hear the phone ring," she asked. "Frank answered it," he told her.

"Oh, that's who he was talking to," she said, then mumbled, "I'll deal with him later."

They talked for a while as she and Isha rotated. The conversation finally started to wind down when she told him, "Call me every other weekend collect. I love you."

"I will and I love you too," he told her.

"Take care, baby, and don't forget to call me," she stressed.

"I will and I won't," he replied.

"Okay. Tell Paul and Jewel I said hello," she added.

"I will," he responded, waiting for her to end the call.

"Bye baby," she said.

"Bye mama," he said and hung up.

When he hung up, he just sat there thinking about their conversation. He looked around the room and noticed cameras, video equipment, and editing material.

"Yeah, this is his dad's room," he thought as he got up to go into the kitchen.

They were all eating when he walked in, "How's your mom?" his dad asked.

"She's fine-" he started to say, but Amie cut in saying, "Sit by me Roman! Sit by me!"

Roman laughed.

"Dang Amie, let him breathe!" Bryan said, frowning.

"She's okay, but I'm tired and not really hungry, Amie," he said, smiling at her.

"Moated!" Bryan said teasing her.

"Shut up!" she shouted.

"Hey!" Paul said as Jewel said, "stop it you two!" looking at them. "But-" Bryan started to say.

"But nothing! Both of you stop and eat your food!" Paul told them. Roman got quiet and said, "I'll see y'all in the morning," looking tired.

"I doubt it. We'll be gone by 7 or 7:30am, so we probably won't see you until four or five o'clock," Paul told him.

"Well, I'll see you then," he said, yawning.

"Excuse me," he said.

"You're excused," Amie sang and giggled. They all laughed.

"Goodnight," he told them.

"Goodnight," they all replied.

"If you need to know where something is let us know," Jewel added "I will. Goodnight," he responded.

"Goodnight," they all said again. Roman went into his room, looked at his suitcases, and decided to unpack tomorrow. He got a change of clothes, some underwear and toiletries out of his bag and went to take a bath. After he finished, he went to bed and went straight to sleep. His first day back in LA.

Roman didn't wake up until noon and when he got up, he went to see if anybody was home. "Nobody," he said aloud and went to the restroom to relieve himself. He washed his hands, brushed his teeth and washed his face. He was ready to unpack but before he did, he went into the den to check out his dad's music collection and as he went through them he saw just what I thought he would see "nothing but oldies." He decided to go and get some of his music out of his luggage. He picked out some Prince and Whodini. He put on some Prince, turned the volume up, emptied his suitcases and began to organize his clothes, shoes, and other stuff. He was almost finished as he listened to "DMSR" by Prince when the phone rang. He turned the volume down on the stereo and went looking for the phone. He found it in the living room.

"Hello," he answered.

"I see you're up now," she said, shuffling papers and looking at schedules as she held the phone between her neck and shoulder. It was Jewel.

He said, "Yeah, I've been up for about an hour now and I'm almost done unpacking."

"Well, your dad told me to call and check on you," she told him. "Are you finding everything okay?" she asked, stapling some papers.

"Yeah, I'm straight," he said.

"Good, and if you get hungry, there's some Pastrami and roast beef in the refrigerator and there's also everything in there you will need to make sandwiches," she told him. "Oh, there's also some fish and chips in there from last night," she added.

"All right," he said.

"Okay, well that's about it and your Dad should be home by 4pm and the kids and I should be home at about 5 or 5:30pm," she told him. "Okay," he said.

"Talk to you later. Bye-bye," she told him.

"Bye," he said and hung up. He turned the volume back up.

He got some roast beef, cheese, tomatoes, lettuce, mayo, and pickles out of the fridge to make him a sandwich, grabbed a bottle of orange juice, and looked through the cabinets and found a bag of Cool Ranch chips. He was bumping Whodini as he fixed his sandwich and when he went to rinse the knife he had used, he noticed the door of the house behind him open up and a female came out in some serious fluorescent colors and she was brown skin with medium length hair, medium height, and a body that was saying something! She was mostly booty and hips. The kind that jiggles when she walks! *Might be nice,* he thought as he watched her walk toward the front and, when he got a closer look, he noticed that she was attractive but not pretty. *Yeah, I might need to hit that,* he thought.

He said, "easy access! Jiggle It, Baby," as he watched her leave he sat down to eat. When his Dad came home, he was on the phone with Noah.

He told him, "Say, I'll call you back, pops just came home."

"What's up, Dad?" he greeted him.

"Oh, I'm good," Paul answered, looking at the mail then asked him "How was your day?"

He told him: "It was cool. I finished unpacking, and I just got off the phone with Noah. He wants me to work with him and Uncle Ron." Paul looked up from the mail and said, "What did you tell him?"

"I told him that I would get back with him," he answered. "I do need some clothes though," he added looking at his father.

Paul shook his head and said, "Well, you know I don't go shopping, but I'm sure Jewel will take you."

"Okay, I'll ask her," Roman said.

"Oh. Here's your key," Paul said, remembering and taking it out of his pocket to give to him.

"Thanks," he said as he took it.

"Did you meet Marsha?" Paul asked him with a smirk.

He said, "Who? Who's Marsha?"

"The girl that lives behind us," Paul told him. "She asked about you yesterday when I came back outside," he said ,watching for his reaction and there it was: interest. *Like father, like son*, he thought as he smiled at him with his eyes gleaming.

"Is that right?" Roman said.

"Yeah. That's right," Paul said laughing, "and I told her you were my son."

"What did she say?" Roman asked.

"He's foinee!" Paul said imitating her and they both laughed.

"Wait a minute" Roman said suddenly, having a thought and asked, "Why didn't you tell me this yesterday?"

"You were asleep, Roman," Paul said flatly.

"Oh," was all he said.

When Jewel and the kids got home, they ate dinner and Roman spent some time with his little brother and sister and all they wanted to do was play. He talked to Jewel later about going to the mall and she said Saturday would be a good time. He was $350 to the good with the $200 that his Aunt Barbara slipped him. Well $300 really because that $50 was going on his extracurricular activities with Noah and with the information his dad just gave him Marsha was definitely on his hit list now.

~

She was at a costume party in King Oaks at a girl named Pepa's house and it was crunk! The DJ was on fire and had been jamming all night playing a lot of fast songs and that's probably why she was ready to go home! That and the fact that she was a little horny and tipsy too! When the DJ switched it up and played a slow song that was one of her favorites, someone behind her asked, "Would you like to dance?"

When she turned around and saw who it was, she giggled and said, "Nice costume."

He laughed too and said, "so is yours," and meant it because she was wearing that suit! She was dressed as Catwoman!

"So, would you like to dance?" he asked again.

"Yeah. I would... Batman." They both laughed and went to find a place on the floor to dance.

"So what's your name?" he asked, holding her waist as they slow danced.

"Catwoman," she replied.

He gave her a look and asked, "Why is your voice so raspy?"

She got offended and said with an attitude, "If you had been yelling and dancing all night to those fast songs you'd be hoarse too!"

He loosened his hands on her waist and told her, "Hold up. I wasn't complaining. I was just wondering."

She noticed it and tried to change the subject by asking, "So what's your name?" while putting his hands back around her waist.

"Can't you tell?" he asked.

She moved her head back to get a better look at him and said, "uh-uh," shaking her head.

He smiled and said, "Batman." She laughed they continued to dance as the slow songs kept playing. They continued to dance when they got more comfortable with each other they began to dance real close, so close that she could feel his pain!

"What's that?" she whispered in his ear.

"Robin," he told her. She chuckled and laid her head on his shoulder.

"Do you wanna go talk somewhere?" he asked. She didn't answer. She kept dancing and then took his hand and started to walk away and led him into another room, but it was crowded. She found a bathroom and locked the door behind them!

"Take your mask off," he told her.

She said, "no," pulled him toward her and kissed him. It was awkward with the mask on, but they didn't care as his tongue played with hers and his hands roamed all over her body. He squeezed her breast and rubbed between her legs saying, "here, kitty, kitty, kitty."

"You want it!" she whispered in her raspy voice.

"Yeah," he responded. She stopped, unzipped her pants, took one of her shoes off and pulled them down and off with one leg out. She didn't have on any panties! He unsnapped his utility belt, let it hit the floor and pulled his pants down to his ankles and asked her again, "Are you going to tell me what your name is?"

Instead of answering, she just pulled him toward her and asked him, "Do you have a condom?"

He pulled one out of his glove and opened it up. He put it on, lifted her onto the counter, slowly slid inside of her and she was wet and a nice fit. He stroked her as she leaned back against the mirror with her legs raised and her feet planted on the counter. He walked over to the wall with her legs cradled in his arms, pressed her back against it, and started going in and out of her slowly as she moaned. As time went on, her movements began to get faster and faster as she enjoyed him stroking her and felt herself about to come.

"I'm coming! I'm coming!" she said breathlessly as he felt himself about to come too and began to thrust deeper and deeper inside of her until he exploded inside the condom. His arms were numb from holding her up against the wall and as he kissed her he slipped out of her and put her down. He pulled the condom on, flushed it and started to get dressed.

"Could you give me a minute?" she asked.

"Yeah," he responded and walked out the door. She locked it and began to clean herself up and get dressed. *What am I doing? I don't even know him?* she said to herself as she looked in the mirror and shook her head.

She let out a deep breath and said, "I gotta get out of here!" When she opened the door, she was glad to see that he wasn't there. She avoided him, found her friends and her ride. She and her friends were walking behind some guys at school when she heard one of them say, "You lying! I'm tellin' you! It tripped me out!" another one said and, "When I came back she was gone! I didn't even get her name!" he said frustrated.

"Here kitty, kitty, kitty!" his boys mocked him and started laughing. She froze!

"What's wrong with you?" one of our friends snapped as she ran into the back of her causing the fellas to turn around.

"What's up, Stace?" Roman asked as she looked at him.

"You!" she said in her mind, "You!"

"Stacey! Stacey!" somebody said.

"Huh? What?" she said as she woke up looking around.

"What were you dreaming about?" Onika asked.

"Uh, I don't know. I can't remember," she said, lying.

"Well, it must have been bad because you're sweating! Try to go back to sleep!" Onika told her.

These dreams have to stop! I can't believe I slept with my sister's boyfriend but he wasn't with her then, she reasoned! *Still, she can't find out and neither can he*, she thought. *Nobody can ever know*, she said to herself as she took a deep breath and tried to go back to sleep.

~

They went to Macy's in the Del Amo Mall and the Oak Tree in Fox Hill Mall. Roman bought some jeans, shirts and other things. He was with Jewel, Bryan and Amie. They had been gone all day and Jewel still hadn't bought anything.

He wondered why, so he asked her, "Where are we going now?" as they left the parking garage at Fox Hill Mall.

"Pic n' Save," Jewel told him as she put on her shades.

"Oh," he said puzzled. When they made it there and went inside, she started sizing clothes.

"She's buying their clothes from here?" he mumbled as he watched her pick out clothes for Amie and Bryan.

She looked at him and said, "Pick out what you want because your dad gave me some money for you."

"Naw, I'm cool. I'll wait until we go back to a mall."

"Okay," she said and kept looking. When they finally left there, they went to get something to eat from Taco Bell. They made it home and their neighbor, "Marsha" was outside.

"Hi, Marsha," Jewel, Amie and Bryan all spoke.

"Hi," she responded.

"What's up?" Roman said to her as he got the bags out of the car. "Hey, nothing," Marsha answered smiling.

"You lookin' good," he told her as his family went inside.

"Thanks," she said, blushing.

"My name is Roman," he told her.

"I know and mine is Marsha," she told him.

"When you get some time, holler at me," he told her, trying to set something up.

"Okay, I will. Bye.," she told him as she held his gaze and walked off.

"Later" he said and went into the house. He put his bags in his room and went into the living room to use the phone because his mind was made up.

"Hello?" Noah answered.

"What's up?" Roman asked.

"Nothing. What's up with you?" Noah asked.

"Chilling but say, let Uncle Ron know that I wanna work with him," he said, getting straight to the point.

"All right. What changed your mind?" Noah asked curiously.

"You don't wanna know," Roman said.

"Yes, I do!" Noah told him.

"Pic n Save," Roman mumbled on the phone.

Noah laughed and said, "oh! You went shopping with Jewel!" "Yeah," he said flatly.

"I thought you knew that's where she shops," Noah told him, still laughing!

"Naw, I didn't know!" Roman said.

"Well, now you do!" Noah said, trying to stop laughing.

Roman was getting pissed! "Look! Just let Uncle Ron know I wanna work wit' him!" he said quickly.

"All right. I will. Peace," Noah said, still laughing as Roman said, "Later" and hung up the phone.

"Roman your food is on the table," Jewel called out.
"Here I come," he said and went to the kitchen.

CHAPTER IX

"Is it going to hurt?" Marsha asked, looking scared as he prepared to enter her without a condom.

"Naw," he said smoothly, ready to knock her off and as he tried to push himself inside of her she screeched, "Roman wait! Wait!" as she felt pain and her eyes widened.

"Shh-" he said, trying to calm her and put her at ease. He wanted to bust her cherry, and just as he put her at ease he heard his dad say, "Roman!" outside his door as he started turning the knob, but it was locked! They both jumped up and scrambled to get dressed! "Hurry up!" he whispered as his dad banged on the door saying, "Open this door!"

"Go out the window!" he told her, sliding it open before his dad could open the other door that didn't have a lock on it and Roman had a highboy against it just in case and it worked because it bought him some time! She jumped out the window, and he closed it! He laid down and acted like he was asleep just as his dad pushed his way in his room!

"What are you doing in here!" Paul demanded.

"I was sleeping," Roman said groggily as if he had just woken up. Paul looked at him and said, "move!" as he reached over him, pulled the curtain back, looked out the window and saw nothing!

"I know I heard voices in here!" Paul said, looking through the closet and under the bed.

"You probably heard me snoring," Roman lied, trying not to laugh and asked, "Why are you home so early?" trying to change the subject.

"I had something to do, so I took off early," Paul told him, studying him and knowing that he was up to something. *But what?* he thought, looking at him.

"What!" Roman said, laughing under his intent gaze.

Paul told him, " I know you were up to something! I'm sure of it," he told him.

"No I wasn't! You're tripping, dad!" he said, laughing.

"Well, why was the door locked and the highboy against the other door?" he asked.

"Because I was getting dressed earlier and didn't want anybody to walk in on me and I forgot to unlock it" he lied quickly.

Paul looked at him.

I know you! I ain't no dummy, playa! Roman thought, looking at his dad.

Paul let it go for now and said, "Come in the living room and help me with these speakers."

"All right," Roman said and followed him into the living room. He saw Marsha pass by the window as they were fixing the speakers and winked at her mouthing, "next time," as his dad soldered wires not having a clue.

He had finally hooked up with Marsha and knocked her off and was doing it right now as she held her legs up and let him thrust inside of her hard. It was like Bobby Womack said in that song "Love has finally come at Last": "Just like a tender young virgin/ in her first love affair/ the more she did it/ the more she seemed to want it! Want it! Want it!" and that was Marsha's case because every day for the past week, he had been knocking her down and she couldn't get enough of it. Every morning that she saw his parents and the kids leave, she would call and tell him to open the door because she was coming over. She had given him head today for the first time, but right now they were on the living room floor and she was riding him as he guided her hips. She had her eyes closed in pleasure as she rode him and then she opened them and looked into his eyes as she placed her hands on his chest and grinded into him. They did this every day, and she liked it. When she finally came, she leaned over and collapsed on top of him, kissing his neck and rolling on his stick!

"I'll do anything for you!" she whispered in his ear as she brought him to climax!

"We'll- see!" he grunted as he came hard and thought, with her, *I'll never have to worry about getting my row out.* "Easy Access."

~

Casey had been talking to Craig on the phone a lot lately and spending time with him at band camp for the past month and she was really beginning to like him and the more time she spent with him the less she thought about Roman. Stacey had been telling her to forget about Roman and focus on Craig but it was hard because Roman had been calling her but when they talked they only argued, like now. She was on the phone with him and was beginning to think that her sister was right.

"So what have you been doing?" he asked.

She sighed and said, "Nothing, just going to Carrollette Camp and practicing with the band. What about you?" she asked just to make conversation.

He smiled on the phone and said, "Oh, I'm chillin'! Just working with my uncle, vibing with my Dad and spending time with my little brother and sister."

"Oh that sounds nice," she said flatly and he picked up on it. "What's wrong with you?" he asked, frowning.

"Nothing," she mumbled.

"Casey what's up? You don't wanna talk to me?" he asked, getting straight to the point. Silence.

Then: "it's not that," she said unconvincingly.

"Well, then what is it?" he asked again.

"I don't know!" she said frustrated.

"Are you seeing Craig?" he asked her and her eyes went wide with surprise as she said, "What!"

"You heard me. Are you seeing Craig?" he said evenly. She held the phone and played with the cord as he called her name, "Casey!" "I'm here!" she quipped.

"Well, answer me," he told her.

"Yes, Roman! I'm seeing Craig!" she blurted out impatiently. "That's all you had to say. I understand and hey, I love you," he said cooly.

"I love you too," she said quietly and meant it.

"Well, I'm about to go. You be sweet," he told her.

"I-" she started but he cut her off and told her.

"Just leave it alone, Casey. Leave it alone." She paused and said, "bye" and he returned it and hung up. After she hung up, she wondered if she had made a mistake as she sat on her bed thinking. The doorbell rang and then Stacey said, "Casey! You got company! Craig's here!" She got up, looked in the mirror, let out a deep breath, and headed toward the living room.

"Hi," she said smiling when she came into the living room and tried to hide the emotions she was really feeling.

~

"So what's up?" Paul asked him as they drove to Anaheim to see the Raiders play today and Roman was looking forward to it because he had been working with his Uncle Ron.

"Nothing. Just chillin' and waitin' on my check," Roman answered. He had sanitized restrooms, cleaned offices and stripped and waxed floors all week!

"I heard that so how much do you think you made? Paul asked him. "Enough," was all Roman said.

Paul glanced at him and chuckled. "So you're not going to tell me?" he asked.

"No sir!" Roman said laughing. Paul laughed too and said, "I taught you well" and shook his head. When they made it to the stadium, it was hard to find a parking space but after some maneuvering they found one. They filed in with everybody else, got something to eat and found their seats to watch the game.

Later as they were driving home Paul asked, "Why don't you hang out with Jewel tomorrow?"

Roman looked perplexed as he asked, "Huh? What for?"

Paul glanced at him, "Well, she is going to be your stepmom soon so I think you should get to know her better."

"Okay, but what are we going to do and where are we going to go?" he asked, still perplexed.

"You can go to work with her tomorrow since you don't have anything to do tomorrow," Paul suggested. Roman looked surprised as he thought about Marsha. He did have something planned for tomorrow: "Marsha." He hadn't seen her in a week because he had been working and was looking forward to some "me time or them time" as he called it. *Dang,* he thought and sighed as he said "all right" but smiled when he had another thought. He could just see her Tuesday. He and Jewel talked and listened to Rick Dees in the morning on KISS FM as she drove to work. They had just dropped Bryan and Amie off and he was still thinking about what had happened when they dropped Amie off. *That was a trip* he thought and smiled because one of the employees at the preschool was giving him action. Her name was Rochelle and she made sure that Roman spoke to her and that she introduced herself to him. She was tall with dark brown eyes, very dark skin, pretty teeth, slim, sexy and had her hair in braids. *Doable* he thought and chuckled as he remembered what Amie did and said.

Jewel looked at him and asked, "What's so funny?"

"I was thinking about what Amie did," he told her, laughing.

"Come on, Man," she smiled and said, "Yeah, I should have told you she watches everything and misses nothing."

"I see that now!" he said with it still on his mind. When Rochelle introduced herself to him Amie watched her like a hawk and after they exchanged greetings Amie motioned for him to *come here* with her little finger so she could tell him something.

When he bent down, she cupped her hands over his ear and whispered to him, "I think she likes you," and glanced at Rochelle to make sure she couldn't hear what she said.

Roman smiled and cupped his hands over her ear and whispered, "I think you're right." Amie giggled, smiled at their secret, kissed him and Jewel and waved goodbye to them as Rochelle walked her inside.

"Ro-chelle," he said and smiled.

"Huh?" Jewel said as she made her exit.

"I didn't say anything," he lied.

~

Faye stood in the doorway of Isha's room watching her sleep and wondering what was really going on with her daughter. She was furious when Isha told her she wasn't going to college but had calmed down now since Isha had a job, but something still was not right and she believed she had finally put her finger on it. She hoped that she was wrong, but in her heart she knew that she was right. She walked over to the bed, sat down and brushed Isha's hair away from her face.

"Isha, Isha wake up," she said, shaking her gently.

She stirred mumbling: "hmm, what? and then when she opened her eyes and saw her mother sitting there she said: "Mama, what's wrong?" closing her eyes back and stretching.

"Isha, we need to talk," Faye said firmly but quietly, causing Isha to stop and open her eyes mid-stretch.

"What about?" she asked nervously, avoiding her mother's eyes.

"I think you know," Faye stated matter-of-factly.

"No I don't, Mama" she said, then Faye asked, "Isha, when was your last period? Are you pregnant?" Isha's eyes widened and she gasped!

"What?" she said, surprised by her mother's question!

"You heard me!" Faye said sternly, leaving Isha speechless as she just looked at her mom and tears filled her eyes and fell freely down her cheeks!

"Mama...I-I didn't know how to tell you," she stammered and cried!

Faye was in shock and wishing that she had been wrong! Faye started shouting, "Oh my God! I knew it! Isha why! I can't believe it! That's why you didn't go to college! I'll be a-" but stopped when Isha broke down and confessed, "Mama, I'm sorry and I'm scared!" sobbing loudly. Faye looked at her and the state she was in and forgot all about her anger and became concerned for her daughter! Her oldest child, who needed her at a time like this so she did the only thing a real mother would do and reached out, hugged her and tried to calm her down! She kissed her on her forehead and told her: "We'll get through this Isha and everything is gonna be okay! Trust me and stop crying because it's not good for the baby!" as she began to cry too.

"I am sorry!" Isha told her sobbing.

"Hush!" Faye told her trying to comfort her and added, "oh! You know you're still going to college right!" as she pushed her back gently and looked in her face.

Isha nodded her head and said, "Yes ma'am, and I love you, Mama!" as tears continued to fall down her face.

"I love you too baby!" Faye told her and hugged her again. When they both calmed down, they talked about everything from doctor's appointments to her getting enrolled in school next fall, to discussing the father, calling her dad and getting everything ready for the baby.

"Hmph, I can't believe it. I'm gonna be a grandmother," Faye said, shaking her head and Isha dropped her head in guilt. When Faye saw this, she took Isha's chin, raised her head up, looked at her and said, "Hey. I hope it's a girl" and smiled.

"Me too, Mama" Isha said, smiling for the first time and crying not in fear but in happiness.

~

"I'm here to pick up my son, Roman Chance," Jewel told the officer at the desk. She couldn't believe she was in a police station to pick him up. She and Paul got worried when he didn't come home from school and then they received a phone call from the police informing them that their son was at the police station and they would release him into their custody. Paul didn't come because he was afraid of what he might do, so he sent Jewel. She hoped that he would be calm when she and Roman made it home. He rarely resorted to whooping, but in this case she wouldn't be surprised. She looked at her watch again and wondered what was taking so long as she paced back and forth with her heels clip-clopping and biting her bottom lip in anxiety and just when she walked toward the desk she saw an officer escorting him to the desk. He looked worn as he walked toward her with his hands in his pockets.

"Are you okay?" she asked him anxiously, searching his eyes. "Yeah, I'm good," he replied then asked, "Where's dad?"

"He's at home" she answered with a *and you should be glad* look and he was glad!

"Is he pissed off?" he asked, already knowing the answer. She let out a lengthy breath and said, "Yes." She looked around and said "Let's get out of here" before touching his arm and going out the door and into the parking lot. When they got closer to home, he got nervous. He hoped that Amie and Bryan were asleep so they wouldn't see or hear their dad trip with him. When they entered the house Bryan and Amie were sitting on the couch with Paul watching television and he said, "dang" under his breath. Amie heard the door close and peeped to see who was coming.

When she saw Roman, she asked, "Roman, where've you been? Did you stay at school this late?" and jumped off her dad's lap and ran toward him.

"Bryan and Amie come with Mommy so Daddy and Roman can talk," Jewel told them to save him from having to lie to them or answer questions from Bryan.

"Mom!" they both whined.

"You heard your mother! Go!" Paul said, pointing to his bedroom. "Are you in trouble?" Bryan whispered, looking at his brother for an answer.

"No, we just need to talk," Roman told him, hoping he wouldn't ask him anything else. Bryan looked at him, then followed his mother. She took them in her bedroom, closed the door and turned the volume up on the television. Paul looked at him and said nothing, and Roman knew that he was pissed off!

"Anxious to get this over with," Roman said, "Dad, I'm sorry". "Shut up!" Paul said firmly, trying hard to contain his anger. Roman got quiet and Paul said, "I didn't know where you were for hours then we called your Uncle Lawrence and he said that you never came to his house after school and all I could think about was what could I tell your mom if something had happened to you! I didn't know if somebody had killed you, robbed you or what!" Paul was getting angrier just thinking about it and he wasn't finished! "Then I find out that you're being held at a police station for possession of marijuana on a school campus!" Paul shouted then asked angrily, "What is your problem man?" but Roman didn't answer and Paul said, "I brought you here to keep you out of trouble not for you to get into trouble!"

"Dad-" he started to say but Paul cut him off saying, "Man just shut up! I don't want to hear it! I'm so pissed at you right now that I could-!" Paul stopped, took a deep breath and said, "Man, just get out of my face!" Roman went to his room and closed the door. He laid on his bed and thought about what happened. He and two guys were sitting on a bench in the smoking area at school on the quad at Crenshaw smoking a joint when a security officer crept up on them! They got rid of the joint and hid the sack of bud but not the smell as the security officer's question told them. "Is that weed I smell?" he asked, sniffing the air. No, we were just smoking cigarettes" Roman answered and the other two boys nodded their heads in agreement. "Yeah okay. Then you three won't mind coming with me right now" he said sarcastically, and it was more of a statement than a question so they got up and followed him. He took them to the vice principal's office and made them wait outside with another security officer while he explained the situation. He came back out and escorted them one by one until he got to Roman who was the last one. When he walked into the office the vice principal immediately asked him, "Where are the drugs?"

Roman said, "What? What drugs?" feigning ignorance.

"The drugs that you have on you," he stated matter-of-factly.

"I don't know what you're talking about," Roman answered in a sincere tone, hoping he bought it.

"Okay... so you wouldn't mind if we searched you," the vice principal said slowly.

"I don't have a problem with it so do what you have to do.," Roman answered smartly, knowing he had them beat. Now it would be different if they had dogs he thought to himself. "Search him," the vice principal told the security officer, and he walked over to

Roman and told him to take everything out of your pockets, put it on the desk, then take a step back, spread your legs and place your hands up over your head. Roman complied and the security officer searched him thoroughly and even made him take off his shoes but when he was done he found nothing and looked at the vice principal in confusion and said, "He's clean."

Roman smirked and said, "Can I go now?"

The vice principal looked at him for a few seconds and then said "Not yet. Drop your pants." Roman's heart sank, but he kept a straight face and said, "what!" indignantly. "You heard me. I said drop your pants," he repeated with a smirk of his own and that set Roman off because now he knew those marks had snitched on him! *Busters!* he thought with his mind racing, trying to think of a plan but coming up with nothing! "You can either do it now or when the police come," he said, taunting him and snapping him out of his thoughts. Roman looked at him saying nothing then unbuckled his belt, unbuttoned his 501's, and pushed them past his waist. The security officer watched but saw nothing. He frowned at the vice principal like this was a waste, but he motioned for him to hold up and told Roman, "Pull your boxers down."

Roman looked at him like he was crazy and said so: "You must be crazy! Now I know you're tripping!" with a face of defiance.

"Pull them down!" he repeated and after a brief silence, Roman pulled his boxers down to the beginning of his pubic hair revealing a small sack of bud.

"Ah-ha!" the vice principal said with a look of triumph and instructed the security officer to take it and place it on his desk but before he could Roman snatched it out of his boxers, threw it on his desk, told the security officer, "don't bother," then looked at the vice principal and said defiantly, "Now what!"

"Noww, you will go to the security office and be held there until LAPD comes to pick you up and you cannot return to this school without a parent," he told him then asked "understood?"

Roman said smartly, "I do understand English! Understood!" The vice principal leaned forward in his chair and said angrily, "Mr. Gibbs, get him out of my office!"

"Yes sir," he replied and put his hand on Roman's arm and led him out of the office. Later that night, he told his father and Jewel the same story, but flipped it a little when he thought about those marks snitching on him. He told them that when the security officer came one of those busters threw the sack on him, he panicked and stuffed it inside his boxers. He tried to play it off by saying that the bud was not his and it worked to a certain extent but not enough to escape punishment from his dad! He was grounded for a month and it was decided that Jewel would be the one to take him back to school and meet with the vice principal because she didn't have to be at work until 9am.. After the meeting, Roman was glad because he was reinstated in school and he didn't have to receive any corporal punishment like he did in Louisiana. Jewel got down for him and she got into a heated argument with the vice principal and made her position known! She told him her son told her the drugs were not his, so they were not his and she would believe her son over those boys any day because her son does not lie and he has excellent grades! But Roman didn't expect anything less from Jewel! Especially since she got high with him sometimes! "Imagine that!"

This was his second week in detention, and he was waiting to be excused. The detention officer always let them out before the bell rang so they could make it to their homeroom on time. Roman thought about homeroom and wondered why schools in California made 3rd period homerooms, but schools in Louisiana made homeroom separate from all other classes and was at the start of the school day.

138

"You may leave now," the detention officer told them and everybody got up. When Roman walked into his physiology class, the only one there was this chick named Cheyenne who was in detention with him. He had seen her in the smoking area and they had flirted with each other but he had never followed up on it but today would be the day.

"What's crackin', Cheyenne?" he asked.

She looked up at him, sighed and said, "Nothing. I'm just tired of getting detention."

"Well, get to class on time!" he said jokingly.

She cocked her head and said, "o-kay! Who are you to talk! You're in detention every day!" and laughed at him.

Roman laughed too and said, "You're right but you're the only reason I go!" She stopped laughing and gazed at him trying to see if he was telling the truth but Roman was too smooth to give her anything less. He regarded her as she held his gaze and she was very attractive. She was 5 2', with dark chocolate skin, black shoulder-length hair, sexy lips, dark eyes, firm breasts, a small waist, and a round booty. She blushed and said softly, "look at you."

"I'd rather look at you," he told her and pulled out a chair and sat in front of her.

"Is that all?" she asked boldly, letting him know where she wanted this to go.

"Naw. I want to do a lot more," he replied looking in her eyes. She felt the tension and challenged him saying, "Like what?" and he immediately caressed her face, pulled her face to him and kissed her and she welcomed the kiss! He kissed her slowly, caressed her breasts, and squeezed her nipples, which were firm! She moaned and kissed him more aggressively as she stroked his erection through his jeans, but he broke their kiss realizing they had little time and he wanted to be inside of her now! He stood up, took her hand and led her toward the lab area where the tables would shield them, and without saying a word, he unbuckled his belt unzipped his pants, pulled them down to his ankles along with his boxers, and began stroking himself and she just looked at him!

"Talking loud and sayin' nothing," he challenged!

She said, "Hhmph!" with a smirk and began to come out of her shorts. She pulled them down to her ankles, and he stepped between her legs, placed his hands on her booty, lifted her up and eased her down on his erection. He got harder and harder as he began to fill her and she got wetter and wetter as he moved in and out of her as she wrapped her arms around his neck. He wanted to hit it better, but he didn't have time, so he hit it as quick and as hard as he could before the bell rang! He snapped, "dang!" when the bell rang and quickly pulled out of her, placed her back on her feet and stepped from between your legs so they could get dressed! When they were dressed, she was still riding off what just happened and told him, "Roman we need to finish this," looking at him intently!

He told her: "Let's ditch school tomorrow then and when my stepmom drops me off, I'll meet you at the bus stop on Vernon and we'll ride the bus back to my house and finish what we started." "All right," she agreed as the teacher and students started entering the classroom.

Roman smirked and said suggestively, "You better be ready." She smiled and bit her bottom lip as she remembered what just happened and said quietly, "no, you better be ready" with desire in her eyes. "Always!" he said confidently.

~

Roman had on a pair of Levi 501 jeans, a royal blue Dallas Cowboys sweatshirt with a Turkish rope around his neck and a pair of blue and gray Diadoras on his feet while Noah had on a pair of black Guess jeans, a black and gray Raiders sweatshirt with a flat link chain, and bracelet around his neck and wrist and a pair of black and white gangsta' Nikes on his feet as they stood on the corner of Vernon at night waiting on the bus to come. They were tired and ready to make it home. The punishment from his dad was over and they had enjoyed themselves all day! They met Noah's girlfriend and her cousin at a bus stop, went to the mall, did a little shopping, went to the movies, out to eat, and got their drank, and smoke on. They had just left Noah's girlfriend's house on the westside.

Noah started getting hungry and asked Roman, "What time is it?" while looking down the street and hoped the bus wasn't coming. Roman looked at his watch and said, "11:07pm, Why? What's up?"

"I'm hungry, man," Noah said, rubbing his stomach.

"Me too!" Roman said.

"It's all that bud we smoked," Noah told him.

"No doubt! I'm still high!" Roman laughed.

"Well, check this out! I'm about to go across the street to Fat Burgers and get us something to eat so watch for the bus because it's probably the last one!" Noah told him then said, "I won't be long but if you see it coming, let me know!

"Bet," Roman said, and Noah walked across the street. As Roman stood thinking about being off punishment somebody said, "What's up homie?" and when he looked up he saw two dudes in all black staring at him!

"Chillin'" Roman said, wondering how he let these fools walk up on him! Then asked, "What's crackin'?" trying to feel these fools out and keep them talking!

"Just maxin' and seeing what we can get into," one of them said. When one of them said that, Roman looked at them, sized them up and hoped these fools weren't strapped because he wasn't! The other one looked down at Roman's feet and told him, "Those are some nice shoes, homie."

"Is that right?" Roman said slowly, seeing what was about to jump off!

"Yeah," they both said as the tension began to build!

"What's up!" Noah said as he came and stood beside Roman! They looked at him then at each other and one of them said, "just mobbin' but we about bail" realizing the situation just changed. He nodded at his partner and they walked off. When they were gone, Noah said, "here" and gave Roman his food.

Roman said, "I'm glad you came! I think those fools were about to try to jack me for my shoes!"

"Yeah! I saw when they stepped to you and tried to hurry up!" Noah told him as they both looked through their bags to make sure their orders were right!

"That's what's up!" Roman said and held his fist out to his cousin. "You know it!" Noah said and gave him dap!

"Look! Here comes the bus!" Roman said while eating some fries. "It's about time!" Noah said ready to get home. They both laughed! They were talking and laughing when they got on the bus but they both knew nothing about what just happened was funny because people were getting jacked and killed for their shoes every day! In five more minutes, who knows how that situation would've played out!

"Roman! Roman!" Amie said quickly, running to her brother and hugging his waist as he closed the door. Ron and Noah had just dropped him off.

He put his bag down and picked her up, "Hey beautiful!" he said as he laughed and kissed her on her cheek. "Did you miss me?" he asked her, pressing his cheek against hers.

"For sure!" she mimicked him and they both started laughing. "Amie, you're a mark!" Bryan told her because he was jealous of the attention she was getting.

"No I'm not!" she said.

"Bryan, don't call her that," Roman told him as he walked into the living room and sat beside him on the couch with Amie.

"She is a mark!" Bryan said glaring at Amie.

"No, I'm not! You're a buster!" she shouted at him.

"Hey! Hey! Hold up!" Roman said, ready to put an end to this now. He looked at Bryan and asked him "Bryan, do you love me?" Bryan looked at him and said, "yeah!" then he turned to Amie and asked "Amie, do you love me?"

She smiled and told her big brother, "yes," then rolled her eyes at Bryan.

Roman said "Okay! No More Fighting!" pointing at them then said, "Hug each other." Amie frowned and Bryan said, "yeah right!" sarcastically. Roman got up and said, "All right! I'm out of here!" They looked at each other and both said, "Wait! Wait!" grabbing his arms. He sat back down and smiled as Amie crawled over to him and hugged Bryan then he said, "now hug me" and they both did. Jewel was watching the whole thing and shook her head in amazement at how well he handled them. She could see that they loved one another very much.

"Isn't that sweet," she teased them, making her presence known and causing them to laugh.

"Hey Jewel. Where's Dad?" Roman spoke and asked her.

"He's out with some friends and will probably be back after you guys are asleep," she told him then added, "speaking of which, you two, let's go to bed," looking at Amie and Bryan.

"Mom!" they both whined.

"I don't want to hear it! Now hug and kiss your brother and tell him goodnight!" she said adamantly. They did what she said and went to their room to wait on Roman.

"Are you hungry?" Jewel asked before going into the kitchen.

"No, I ate earlier so I'm going to go take a shower and go to bed, so I'll be ready for school tomorrow," he told her and stood up to go to his room.

"Okay, Goodnight" she told him.

"Goodnight," he replied.

"Oh Roman," Jewel said, peeking her head out of the kitchen. "Yeah?" he asked.

"You received some mail yesterday, and I put it on your dresser," she told him.

"All right, thanks," he said.

"You're welcome," she told him and went back to what she was doing. When he came out of the shower, Roman put out his clothes for tomorrow and spent some time with Bryan and Amie before they fell asleep then he looked on his dresser and saw two letters. One was from his mom and the other was from… Jennifer Swartz. He smiled and said, "So that's her last name. Imagine that." He read the letters and when he was finished he had received some good news and some not so good news!

He was off this weekend sitting in the living room watching a movie as he thought about his mom's letter again that let him know Isha is pregnant and come to find out his dad knew too because the day after reading the letter he told Paul and Paul shook his head and told him that was why he was out so late last Sunday because Faye called and told him! Paul told him he was angry and hurt and couldn't believe it! Out of all people Isha Roman thought and felt the same way, but after reading his mom's letter that changed when she told him Isha had been through enough trying to hide her pregnancy from her and needed his support and not his criticism. She also let him know the baby would be born in March. He exhaled loudly as he kept pondering his mom's letter because this is the weekend he usually calls home and he didn't know what he would say but after giving it some more thought he smiled at him becoming an uncle and having a nephew or niece. "Uncle Roman!" he said aloud and laughed as he grabbed the remote and turned off the movie! He got up, went into his room and read Jennifer's letter again to put his mind and eyes on something else. In her letter she apologized for not writing to him sooner and hoped he hadn't forgotten about her but if he had, here are some pictures to remind him who she is and how she looks! As he looked at the pictures again, he admired her green eyes, pretty smile and banging body! She had a mischievous smile on one of them as she posed in a two-piece bathing suit and another one where she had on some tight jeans and a baby tee and it made him wonder if he would ever get a chance to touch her body! He got up, grabbed a pen and paper and began to write to her and when he was finished he called home and talked to his mom, Isha and Frank. Remembering his mom's letter, he told Isha he couldn't wait for his nephew or niece to be born and was looking forward to becoming an uncle. That made Isha happy, and the call went smooth! After hanging up he thought about Marsha because his dad, Jewel and the kids were visiting some friends in the valley and he was home all by himself! He picked up the phone, called her, and she picked up on the second ring. "Hello?" she answered.

"Hey. Are you busy?" he asked.

"Hi and no. What's up?" she said.

"Come over," he said.

"I'm on my way," she said and hung up.

"Easy access," he thought as he went to unlock the door.

~

"It's about time we got together," Rochelle said as she sat on the sofa and took her purse off her shoulder.

"I know right," he said as he put on some music and then came and sat beside her on the sofa. "Do you want anything to drink?" he asked her as he put his arm around her.

She shifted a little and said: "all I want is you" as she put her hand on his thigh and moved toward him for a kiss. She rubbed her hands up and down his back and moaned as their kiss got intense and Roman grabbed her waist to let her know he wanted her to stand up. She moaned and broke their kiss, stood up, and took her shirt off, then Roman unhooked her bra and she pulled it off without missing a beat. She kissed him again and Roman felt for the button on her jeans, undid it, unzipped her jeans, and then stepped back and took his shirt and shorts off and stood in front of her naked and at attention. She looked at him and her eyes got big but she grabbed on to her jeans and pulled them down, shimmying out of them. When they came down she stepped out of them and took her panties off. Roman took her hand and led her to his dad's bedroom. He pulled the comforter and sheets back and told her to lay down then he got in the bed beside her and traced her body with his hands and as he got harder, he got on top of her and kissed and sucked her lips, her neck and her breasts, and she began to moan. He continued until he thought she was far from being dry and raised up on his left arm and prepared to enter her, but when he did, he met resistance and she hissed at the same time! He stopped, looked at her and stated the obvious, "you're a virgin!" She looked in his eyes with want and need and said, "Yes and I want you to be my first!" Roman couldn't believe it, not that she was a virgin but the thought of how many virgins he had broken in and she was 19 years old! She brought him out of his thoughts when she stroked him and said, "Come on, Roman." She didn't have to tell him twice! He took his time and tried to break through again and when he finally did, the pain she first felt turned to pleasure and he showed her his claim to fame. He was enjoying her tightness, and she was enjoying the feelings he was giving her and he was going slow and being gentle with her so she could get used to him and when she did, he started banging her and hitting that bottom. "This feels so good Roman! Don't stop!" she cried as he kept laying the pipe and it did feel good! So good that suddenly he felt himself about to cum and so did she because she came right along with him! "Ahhh-ouuuu," she screamed as she came! After she came, she was panting and trying to catch her breath and when she did, she moved her fingers up and down his back and kissed him repeatedly. He smiled at her affection. She smiled back and told him, "That was nice Roman and I'm glad you're my first."

"You're welcome," he said jokingly.

She laughed and asked, "okayyy. So what's next?"

He took a deep breath, exhaled and said "Well, judging by the feel of things under us and between us, you need to take a shower and I need to clean this up and wash these sheets in the washer." She gasped and her eyes widened when she realized what he meant and apologized saying, "Roman, I'm so sorry!" He laughed it off and said, "It's cool. Go take your shower and I'll take care of this." She relaxed and went to take a shower and picked up her clothes on the way while Roman got up and put the sheets and towels in the washer. When he was finished, he joined her in the shower. When they got out of the shower he told her to go to his bedroom while he put the towels they just used in the washer too. When he walked into his bedroom, she was ready and he was too.

CHAPTER X

"Did you get the pictures?" Jennifer asked teasingly as she talked to Roman.

"Yeah, I got them and you look good," he replied looking at her pictures again.

"Have you talked to Isha?" she asked.

"Yeah" he said, proudly smiling as he thought about his new niece. Isha had given birth to a beautiful baby girl in January and he couldn't wait to see her and he told Jennifer so as they continued to talk. "Sooo, when are you coming home?" she asked, trying to give him a hint that she wanted to see him.

"Why?" he asked jokingly.

"Because, I want to see you," she said sincerely.

"I want to see you too," he told her wondering if he should string her along or just go ahead and tell her what was happening because every conversation they had she would mention him coming home and after Summer was born his mom and sister kept telling him she needed to see her uncle in person and they told him Summer is so beautiful! His little niece Summer Chance he thought with a smile as he listened to Jennifer go on and on.

Yeah, it was time, he thought as she said, "so I was-" but he said "Jennifer," cutting her off and she stopped and said, "huh?" wondering what she had missed.

"Guess what?" he asked.

"What?" she asked, wondering what he was about to say.

"I'm coming home this summer.

"Ahhhhhh!" she screamed and said, "I knew it! I knew it!"

"Ahhhhh!" she screamed again and Roman took the phone away from his ear laughing then asked her, "Are you finished?"

"Roman how long have you known?" she asked to calm down.

"A couple of months," he answered.

"What! Why didn't you tell me!" she yelled into the phone causing him to move the phone away from his ear again. "We've been talking for months," she added wondering why he would do this. He told her, "I know. I was going to tell you, but I wanted it to be a surprise," then asked her, "Are you surprised?" and laughed. "Uhm-yes and it's not funny, Roman!" she quipped.

"I'm sorry. Do you forgive me?" he asked.

"No!" she said, pouting.

"I'll make it up to you" he told her and she asked: "How?" wondering when he was coming home.

"You'll see," he told her and as they continued to talk, he told her the plans of him returning home in June for summer vacation. They made plans to see each other, but he also let her know that he had to spend ample time with his family, especially with his niece!

"I'm serious! Don't let her talk you into staying!" Paul warned him again while they discussed him leaving.

"I won't. I told you that already. It's only for the summer," Roman repeated trying to assure his dad he understood what he was saying but he still wasn't convinced.

"I know your mom and she can be pretty persuasive son," Paul told him.

Roman laughed and said, "I got it just trust me," as he smiled at his dad and held his fist out motioning for him to knock that down and as Paul did he held his thoughts back which were: "He really didn't want him to go".

~

"How does she look Roman?" Isha asked, smiling as he looked in the crib at his niece with a frown on his face and asked, "Who is this white baby?"

"Boyy! My baby ain't white!" she said, smacking him on his arm. He laughed and held his arms up, trying to protect himself as he said, "I'm only kidding."

"You better be," she told him playfully.

"Seriously though, she's a doll, and very beautiful," he replied looking at his niece and touching her face.

"She is," Isha said looking at her daughter proudly.

"Come on. Let's go before I wake her up," he told her, really wanting to hold her in his arms.

Just like old times, Roman thought as he, Gerald, Trey, and Cotton kicked it in his front yard on this sunny day enjoying their summer. "Man, when are you going back?" Gerald asked as they talked. Roman looked at him and said, "Well, I'll probably leave when you guys return to school around mid-August."

"Dang, listen to how you talk!" Trey told him, causing them to laugh.

Roman said, "Don't start homie. I get enough of that from my family."

"Naw, I ain't got no problem with it," Trey told him.

"Yeah, you just sound different," Gerald said.

"Okay, but-" he started, then stopped, and they said, "What?" as they turned to see what he was looking at.

"I know this-" Trey said, but Roman stopped before he could finish saying, "Chill."

"You sure?" Gerald asked.

"Yeah. Just be cool" Roman told them.

"What's crackin', Craig?" Roman asked him when he walked up to them then greeted him with a handshake and a half-hug and the fellas followed suit.

"Aww, I'm just chillin'," Craig said nervously trying to feel the situation out.

"I see you heard I was home. Who told you?" Roman asked him. "Uhh, Isha mentioned it to me yesterday when I saw her at Popeyes," Craig told him.

"Okay," Roman said as a smile came to his face as he looked past Craig, then he said, "Here comes your girl" with a nod of his head amused by the situation.

"Dang! She got her crew wit' her too!" Cotton said, licking his lips. "Hook us up, Craig!" Trey said ready to mack on one of them when he saw Casey and four other chicks walking their way with tight shorts on and baby tees! Casey had her hair in a new style that hid her forehead and framed her face. Casey had a frown on her face but Roman just smiled at her wondering how she would handle this situation. He wasn't tripping because he was kicking it with Jennifer and a few other chicks had rushed him at the skating rink last night so he had a few numbers to play with too.

Casey yelled, "Craig! Come here, Craig!" as she and her crew stopped in the street just short of Roman's house. She motioned for him to come to her with her finger and he looked uncomfortable as he told them: "I'll be back."

"Take your time" Roman told him, laughing to himself.

"Hook us up, Craig!" Trey whispered again before he walked away. "What's up, Casey?" Roman said with a smile as Craig went to her but she didn't answer, so he spoke to her friends and said, "Hello ladies."

"Heyyy!" they responded with smiles and waves and Casey cut her eyes at them and Roman laughed. Casey told Craig something, then he told them, "Hey! I'll check y'all later" and Casey smirked.

"Be cool," Roman told him then looked at Casey and said, "Bye Casey." She gave him a flimsy wave and a smirk.

"Goodbye ladies!" he and the fellas said.

"Bye!" they responded giggling and even made Casey smile.

"Go ahead and bone out with them and I'll catch up with you guys some other time," Roman told them as Casey and her crew started to walk past them. That was all Gerald and Cotton needed to hear! "Later!" they told him, but Trey asked him, "You sho'?" and Roman said, "Yeah, I'm straight. Stay up," as he watched them leave and thought some things never change but some things do as he made sure he had his keys and started walking the other way and as he walked Casey was laughing at her girls talking to the fellas until she glanced back and saw Roman headed the other way toward Idaho Drive *to Jennifer's house* she thought. She frowned for a fleeting second then tried to play it off by laughing and thought he'll be gone soon anyway.

He was licking her snatch and playing with her clit as he slid his tongue in and out of her as she guided his head and after some more oral favor, he traced kisses on her stomach and breast until he reached her lips and gave her a taste of her own flavor, kissing her gently and pulling gently on her tongue. When they broke their kiss, she looked into his eyes and gently pushed him off her and onto his back. Then she straddled him and began placing kisses on his lips, chest, stomach and finally his stick! She took him into her mouth and experienced his wealth. She was taking her time and working him to a nice erection and as she served him he reached down and massaged her nipples, squeezed her breast and after a while whispered, "that's enough" and gently slid out of her mouth. He told her to lie on her back and when he was over here ready to go inside of her, there was hunger in her eyes, and a smile on her face as her blonde hair was splayed across her pillow. He looked in her eyes as he slid inside of her wetness which welcomed him like a glove. She felt good Roman thought when he was all the way inside her and began to stroke her and for every stroke she welcomed him with a roll of her hips and held him close with her arms around his neck and he took his time! They were in this position for a while until Jennifer said, "I wanna be on top." He gave her what she wanted, and she eased down on him and rode him slowly. When she found a rhythm that she liked she rode him until she reached her mission and when she came she fell forward on him and continued to ride him until he came inside of her and she moaned when she felt him release inside of her. When he was limp, she rolled off of him, laid beside him, and began to rub his chest and stomach. She laid her head on his chest and asked him, "How was I?," ready for some pillow talk. "You were good" he told her as he ran his hand over her hair. They laid there talking for a while and suddenly Jennifer got quiet.

Roman noticed it and asked her, "What's on your mind?"

She raised up to look at him and told him, "you and us."

Roman looked in her pretty green eyes and said, "Us sounds good and we're cool. Come here." She did and smiled as he held her in his arms and kissed her cheek.

"You were good," she said as he held her.

"I know," he said, and she said "o-kay!" nudging him playfully.

He laughed and said, "What, it's true."

She laughed and said, "You are too much."

"For sure. Now let's go get something to eat," he said, causing her to laugh.

~

Faye stood in her kitchen smiling as she thought about the blessing of having her son back home as she flipped one of her famous super sized pancakes. She had something on her mind that she wanted to talk to Roman about and she felt this would be the right time. "Good morning mom," he said, startling her.

"Boy!" she exclaimed as she held one hand to her chest and said, "Haven't I told you to quit sneaking up on people!" looking at him like he was crazy because he was laughing and easing up on her to make sure she wouldn't hit him.

"I'm sorry, mom," he told her and kissed her on her cheek.

She smiled and said, "go sit down at the table."

"Okay," he said as Faye turned off the stove and set his plate in front of him then got the butter and syrup and placed them on the table then she went to the cabinet and grabbed a glass then opened the fridge and asked him, "Do you want milk or juice?"

"Milk, please" he said and she smiled. "Thank you, mom," he said as she poured it and sat down to talk to him. He was tearing those pancakes up and Faye just watched him because she was glad he was home.

Roman looked up and asked, "What is it, mom?" wondering why she was looking at him like that smiling.

She shook her head and answered, "Nothing, I just like to watch you eat because you let me know how much you appreciate my cooking. "Oh," he responded and drank some milk. As they continued to talk, Faye took a deep breath and said: "There is something I need to ask you," looking serious now and he furrowed his brow and asked, "What's wrong?" after seeing her expression.

"Well," she said, taking another deep breath and said, "I want you to stay home."

"I'm not going anywhere today," he told her, wondering why she was so serious. She shook her head and fiddled with the lace on one of the placemats and said "No, I want you to stay here and not go back to California."

"What! Mom! No, mom! No! I can't do that to dad and you know Dad is expecting me to come back home and he's already moved into our new house in Compton and my room is ready and on top of that you sent me there!" he told her not feeling this conversation. "I know! I know!" Faye said trying to get a word in

154

edge-wise then said "Wait!" holding her hand up as tears fell from her eyes. "I know what I did but you are my child and I want you to stay here with me, Isha, Summer and Frank! We are your family!" she told him out of anger.

"Mom! Dad, Jewel, Bryan and Amie are my family too!" he responded and shook his head, trying not to get angry out of respect for his mom! "Don't do this mom! Don't do this to Dad!" he said, trying to get through to her.

"I'm not doing anything. I'm just telling you how I feel and I want you to stay here so just think about it. That's all I'm asking," she told him and got up, kissed him and went to her room.

"I can't believe this," Roman said as he sat there stunned wondering what brought this on.

～

"Isha, she is sooo beautiful!" Casey told her as she held Summer in her arms, feeding her as she, Onika, their mom and Isha talked. Isha smiled as she looked at her daughter taking her bottle quietly looking up at Casey.

"How does it feel?" Onika asked, seeing the way Isha looked at her daughter.

Without hesitation, Isha said, "I want to do the best I can for her and I want to give her everything" as a moment of being mothers passed between them.

"That's good, baby, that's how your heart should be for your child," their mom told her as she played with Summer's little earrings.

"Isha, these are some pretty earrings," she added, holding Summer's hand.

"Mama, Roman, and I went to the mall last week to get her ears pierced," Isha told them.

"Did she cry?" Casey asked, taking her eyes off her for a few seconds.

"Girl yeah! She and Roman had a fit!" They all laughed and Summer began to cry.

"Give her to me, baby. She's probably full," Casey's mom told her as she put a towel on her shoulder, reached for her and placed her on her shoulder so she could burp.

"What did Roman do, girl?" Onika asked ready to hear the rest.

"Girlll! After that lady did one ear and she started wailing," Isha started laughing.

"What happened Isha?" Casey asked, wanting to know the rest. "Casey-" Isha started to say, but *bwww* Summer belched, causing them to laugh.

"Mama, she's asleep too" Casey said, looking at Summer and wanting to hold her again.

"Lay her down on her comforter," Isha said and spread it out for her.

"Okay," their mom told her as Isha continued to tell them what happened.

"Then, he said oh no that's enough! One today and another one tomorrow! We'll be back!" Onika and Casey burst out laughing and Casey said loudly, "No he didn't!" and their mom shook her head and said, "shhh!" with a stern look reminding them not to wake the baby up!

"Sorry," they said together and Isha continued, "Yes, he did and mama said, 'boy, have you lost your mind! Let that baby get her ears pierced!': Mom that hurt her!" he said and kissed Summer's face to try and quiet her.

"Awww," Casey and Onika said together.

"Mama went back and forth with him for a minute but she got them done," she told them laughing.

"He's just overprotective of his niece, baby," their mom commented as she rubbed Summer's back then asked, "How is he doing, anyway?"

156

Isha took a deep breath, exhaled and said, "Well, considering what's going on he's all right." Casey and Onika looked at each other and they both asked, "what's going on?"

Isha said, "Mama wants him to stay here, and she doesn't want him to go back to California."

"What!" Onika exclaimed while Casey had a weird look on her face with her mouth open and her mom didn't miss this either.

Their mom sighed and said, "I knew Faye was going to do that, baby.

"How did you know?" Isha asked, confused.

"Because baby- a mother's love and the excitement of having her son home again with no problems and knowing that the time was getting close for him to leave her again had to be weighing on her heart and it's only getting harder and what you just told us confirms it for me and I'd probably do the same thing baby and when you girls get older you will understand." Isha and Onika pondered what she said while Casey pondered something totally different: *Oh my God, he may stay here*!

~

Paul sat there in Roman's room playing his son's guitar. He had bought it for him from a pawnshop in Watts one day when they went to find some speakers. He couldn't believe Roman wasn't coming back, but he knew there was a chance that might happen, especially with Faye involved! He tried to tell him and that was the reason he bought him a one-way ticket and not a round-trip ticket because he knew his ex-wife better than anybody! He laughed to himself as he thought about how persuasive that woman could be with tears and everything.

"Daddy, what are you doing in Roman's room?" Amie asked as she made him put the guitar aside so she could climb on his lap.

"Hey babe. How are you doing?" he asked, smiling as he hugged her and kissed her cheek.

"I'm fine," Amie said, giggling at her dad's affection then asked again, "Daddy, what are you doing in Roman's room?" looking at him and waiting for an answer.

"I was in here thinking, baby" he answered.

"Thinking about what?" she asked, waiting patiently.

Paul sighed and said, "Well, I was thinking about making this room into my office."

Amie's eyes bucked and her mouth formed an *o* and she said, "but where is Roman going to sleep, Daddy?"

He told her: "Amie, Roman is staying in Louisiana," and her eyes bucked again.

"Why?" she asked, not understanding.

"Well, his mother wants him to stay with her and graduate from school in Louisiana," he told her hoping that would be enough for her curiosity, but it wasn't because Amie said, "but-but Daddy, he goes to school at Crenshaw."

"I know Amie, but that's what his mother wants, and that's what he chose to do," he told her and Amie looked off like she was thinking hard about something.

Then she asked: "Daddy, does he love us?"

Paul looked in his daughter's eyes, hugged her and said, "Of course he does, baby, and you should know that too."

"I do, but I miss him too," she said sadly and laid her head on his shoulder.

"Me too, sweetheart. Me too," he said as he picked her up, sat her beside him, and picked up his son's guitar and began to play for Amie.

~

"Hi precious," Roman said to his niece as he changed her Pamper and put some powder on her and when he was finished she just cooed. He was babysitting for Isha while she went to pre-register at Northeast Louisiana University for the fall semester. His mom was at work while Frank was asleep trying to get some rest after working the graveyard shift.

"Are you hungry?" he asked Summer and picked her up, kissed her on her cheek and put her on his shoulder. She cooed as he took her into the kitchen to get her bottle ready. He loved his niece with her little fat self. Her hair was blond like Jennifer's and she had the prettiest gray eyes you'd ever want to see! He always teased Isha about her being near white all the time just to aggravate his sister. Summer made a high-pitch sound that made him laugh as she jumped in his arms!

"Oh, you're having fun, huh!" he said playing with her. He held her up and kissed her on her nose and she made that high-pitched sound again while kicking her legs: this made him laugh more! When her bottle was ready, he put everything else up and went into the living room and fed her and when she was finished he burped her and when she fell asleep he laid her down for her nap.

~

Pecanland Mall had a gang of people there today. People were everywhere, trying to take advantage of all the back-to-school sales and prices. Roman, Isha, and Summer were there picking up a few things for Summer and themselves. He was just leaving Champ's with a pair of Adidas, K-Swiss classics, and some socks and was trying to make it to the meeting spot that he and Isha had agreed on. He didn't want to keep her waiting because they had Summer with them and neither one of them wanted her to get cranky. As he was making his way past people, he saw a real light skin chick coming toward him and she was a proper yellow bone too! She had long silky black hair, brown eyes and a nice body from the front. *She's pretty,* he thought as she got closer and she was wearing a one-piece white short set that you could almost see through! As they got closer to each other, he noticed she was nice up top and had pretty smooth legs. He glanced at our feet and the red nail polish made them real noticeable because of her light skin. *Nice feet* he thought and made his way back up her body. She furrowed her brow when she got closer to him and smiled. She had braces, and he always found braces innocent and sexy!

When they came upon each other they stopped and Roman said, "Hi, how are you doing?"

"I'm fine. How are you?"

"A lot better now," he said, keeping eye contact, and smiling.

She laughed and said, "You don't know who I am, Roman, do you?" and the look on his face was priceless as he tried to remember. She wasn't offended, but, in fact, found it amusing.

She said, "We went to Ouachita Jr. High together. I had bifocals then and a retainer in my mouth and my grandmother taught you in elementary school at Swayze."

His eyes grew wide with recognition, "Angela! Angela Davis!" he said, surprised.

"This is me," she said smiling.

"What's happening?" he said, stepping toward her and giving her a hug.

She smiled and said, "Nothing much. What about you?" and as she was talking he spotted his sister and niece and Isha held her palms out and raised her shoulders as a way of asking what's up then looked at Summer in her stroller letting him know they had to go! Angela looked to see what he was looking at and said, "Isn't that Isha?" and waved.

"Yes. That's her and my niece Summer and that's why I have to go but I would really like to get in touch with you," he said as Isha waved back.

"I'm glad. I'd like that," she said and took out a pen and piece of paper and wrote her number down for him.

"I'll be waiting," she said with a smile as she gave him her number. "Not for long," he said and she laughed and said, "I hope not. Bye Roman."

"Goodbye Angela," he said then hugged her and gave her a kiss on her cheek causing her to blush. He walked toward his sister and niece, looking back at Angela to see how she looked leaving. *Nice and sexy,* he thought. Isha saw what he was doing and was laughing when he made it to them and told him, "You are so silly." He looked down at his niece in her stroller and said, "Summer, is your mother hating?" She just smiled and cooed at him.

Isha said, "Never that. I only congratulate."

"You better," Roman said as they walked toward the entrance and Isha laughed.

Isha was tired and ready to get home! She glanced in her rearview mirror and was glad to see that Summer was asleep after their day at the mall. She would usually ride with her top down but had it up today because of Summer.

Roman was sitting next to her bobbing his head to a song on the radio when he asked, "Sis, would you drop by Jennifer's house so I can see if she's home.

"All right," Isha said with no hesitation. They rode past their house and Century Boulevard and came to a stop sign on Idaho Drive and when Isha went to turn right she said, "Whoa! Who is that Man?" as her turn signal blinked. He looked and there was some guy leaning on a blue Camaro in Jennifer's driveway with her standing beside him laughing and talking.

He looked at her and said, "I don't know. Let's go see." She looked at him and thought, "okay" as she turned the wheel. When they turned into Jennifer's driveway she and the guy looked and he asked her, "Who is that?" while her eyes widened at the sight of Roman but she recovered quickly.

"Don't leave yet," Roman told her before he got out.

"No doubt," she said, hoping nothing was about to jump off, especially with her baby in her car. Jennifer waved at her and Isha gave her a plastic smile and wiggled her fingers.

"Hey," Roman said and kissed her .

"Hi," she said and quickly introduced the guy to him.

"Roman, this is Keith and Keith, this is my boyfriend Roman."

The dude Keith cleared his throat, extended his hand and said, "What's up?"

"What's happening?" Roman said and shook his hand. Jennifer just watched and so did Isha.

Keith looked at Jennifer then at his watch and said, "well, I'd better go. I'll see you when the semester starts."

"Okay be safe," she told him and glanced at Roman.

"Nice meeting you," he told Roman, and he said, "same here," with a firm handshake. Roman nodded at Isha and she understood. She backed out and left then Keith left and Jennifer waved at him.

She looked at Roman and asked, "Do you wanna come in?"

"Nah, I'm good. Let's stay out here," he told her, wondering if he was going to get the truth. "So who was that?" he asked.

She sighed and said, "let's sit down," and walked toward the chairs in front of her house with her arms folded across her chest and as he walked behind her, he couldn't help but notice her nice butt and legs. When they sat down, he said, "So tell me."

Jennifer wasn't the type to play games, so she told him the truth: "Roman, that was my ex-boyfriend from the school I attended in Lafayette and he lives in Richwood. He has plans to attend NLU this fall and was asking me what electives do I think he should take."

"I see," Roman said, then asked, "So, what's his interest in you? Is he trying to be friends or more than friends?" thinking like a man. "I really don't know," she told him.

"Do you want to know?" he asked.

She looked flustered as she said, "Roman, he's a friend and only a friend."

"Okay. We both have friends," he said. She sighed again and asked, "Are you mad?"

He told her, "no, as long as we have an understanding with each other about our relationship we're good."

She got up, stood in front of him, took his hands and asked him again: "Do you wanna go inside?" then looked into his eyes and kissed him. He looked at her and said: "Let's go."

~

The school year had been going well for Roman and he hadn't been in any trouble. He was backstage right now with Trey, Gerald and Cotton getting ready for the pep rally. The curtains were closed, and the auditorium was packed as Tonya was letting him know what they were going to do and how they were going to come out.

"We got this. You just do your part," he told her with a smirk. "O-kay!" she said, imitating him and shaking her head as she fixed his clothes. Tonya was captain of the cheerleaders and she and Roman had kicked it for a minute but it didn't work out because he was a playa'. She tried to change him but couldn't and when she understood that she realized they were better off as friends than lovers and that was safer for her heart she remembered as her squad helped Trey, Cotton, and Gerald with their clothes too. When Roman told her what they wanted to do, she was all for it and came up with something they could do too! This was their senior year, and they were going to enjoy it to the fullest! The pep rally was about to start! The principal opened up in prayer and a short speech, then Tonya and her squad walked out onto the stage and the auditorium went crazy! Students were clapping, whistling and screaming as the girls took the stage! They were dressed like guys and not just any guys! They were dressed like Roman, Cotton, Gerald, and Trey! They all had on 501's, white tees and sneakers and something that belonged to one of the fellas! One had on Trey's jacket, Tonya had on Roman's Turkish rope, another one had on Gerald's glasses and another one had on Cotton's hat. They were lined up at attention with Tonya facing them and she yelled, "yo fellas!"

"What's up!" the girls responded in a supposedly deep voice then Tonya yelled.

"Who you wit?" and they said "You knowww!"

She said it again, "Who you wit?" and they said "eighty-Six!" "What!" she yelled.

"Eighty-six!" they said again and when they did Roman, Trey, Cotton, and Gerald came out saying 80-80-80-80-6-6! 80-80-80-80-6-6! And the students went wild, especially the senior class because they had on the cheerleader's uniforms representing their senior class! They were still shouting when Roman said, "Who are we?" and they answered, "Bulldogs!" "Who are we?" They answered, "Bulldogs" again! Then Roman had the fellas line up and he said, "READY! And they all said together, "OKAY!" Then he led the first cheer saying "Pep! Come on now! Pep! Come on now! Pep! A little louder! Pep! A little louder!" and they rocked that without any reservations of their masculinity as the fellas were dancing and stomping and Roman did a split and it erupted and everybody went wild! They were crunk!

Everybody was talking about the pep rally, and Roman was still high off the energy from it!

"Yeah that was cool," he thought as he walked out of his history class.

"Hey Roman," Wendy said as she came up beside him.

"What's up?" he asked.

"Can I talk to you for a minute?" she asked, holding her books to her chest.

"Yes, come on" he said as they reached the stairs and stood on the landing. Wendy was a sweet, beautiful chick. She was a very petite yellow bone with light brown eyes, rose-colored lips, long black pretty hair with humps and bumps in all the right places. But she was always standoffish with him before he left, but seemed to want his attention now.

It was a trip how one year could change things, he thought as he waited for her to say what she wanted to say. Casey passed them and glanced with a frown. He shook his head and kept his attention on Wendy.

"Are you going to the homecoming coronation?" she asked looking up at him.

"I don't know yet," he said, tripping off this because she wasn't the only one who had asked him. In fact, Casey had even asked him because she and Craig were having problems so he was going with somebody else and two other chicks had asked him too. One was on the basketball team and another was on the track team and a few others had asked, but he had already asked this female named Janay and she was tight! She was a sexy yellow bone with shoulder length curly black hair with highlights, dark bedroom eyes, light freckles and she has a twin sister. She told him she'd think about it and he'd told her that was cool but was seriously considering going with Wendy right now!

"Well, Roman?" Wendy asked.

"What?" he said, giving her his attention again.

"Would you like to escort me?" she asked with a smile.

"Could I get back with you?" he asked.

"Yeah, but don't take too long," she said already knowing other girls had asked him but she didn't care.

"I won't," he told her with a chuckle and she smiled as they headed to their drama class. Janay saw them and wondered what they were talking about as she watched them leave.

"I hope she knows he's going to the coronation with me" she thought with a smirk. She had made her decision when he asked her but just wanted to make him wait which may not have been the right decision she thought as she watched them walk away.

"Do you still wanna take me to the coronation?" she asked when he answered the phone.

He laughed and said, "yes," wondering if she saw him and Wendy talking today.

"Good," she said and smiled even though he couldn't see her.

"Just let me know the color of your dress so I'll know what kind of tuxedo I'll need," he told her.

"I will and we'll talk more when I see you at school, she replied. He looked at the time, sighed and told her, "All right, let me get off this phone so I can take a shower and go to bed."

"Can I come?" she said seductively.

"Anytime," he told her.

"Bye Roman" she said and laughed.

~

"I told you not to go over there, didn't I! Didn't I!" he told her again, pissed off.

"I know, Roman! Shut up!" She yelled, not wanting to talk about it! "Shut up! No, you shut up!" he told her not trying to hear it.

"All you had to do was listen to me! I told you, Janay, Casey is not your friend! But did you listen to me? No. Now look what happened," he told her, not caring about her feelings.

"I know! I know, Roman!" she repeated, not believing what happened. They were in their last week of practice for the coronation and Casey invited Janay and Ranay over to her house to chill after school so they could come back to practice together since they were all in the coronation. When Janay told Roman, he told her, "Do not go over there because Casey is not your friend." "Roman! You don't own me! I wanna go so I'm going!" she said smartly.

"I just wanted to let you know I'll be in the neighborhood," she told him and put her hand on his cheek. He moved her hand, shook his head and walked away. Well, Casey got her drunk and while she was drinking, she was falling into Casey's trap! Ranay was in the main house, kicking it with Onika and Stacey who was home visiting from college while Casey and Janay was in the guest house. Roman didn't like the idea of Casey messing over Janay at his expense! When they made it to Carroll High School gymnasium Janay was sick and pissy drunk! She couldn't even practice and Ranay had to help her stand! Roman just looked at her and shook his head because all she had to do was listen to him and Casey stood back watching knowing he was pissed! She winked at him and smiled just to let him know that it was on purpose. Janay went into the girl's restroom in the gymnasium's lobby and threw up, and when she came back out she looked at Roman with sadness in her eyes. Somehow the principal got wind of the situation and came to check it out and after seeing Janay and talking to her, he told her "She was out of the coronation, suspended for three days and she had to get off the school campus now!" Onika told Roman she would take Janay home. Janay was mad and wondered how she let this happen right under her nose! She didn't know Casey like she thought she knew her Roman thought and to add insult to injury he didn't have a date now for the coronation or so he thought because Wendy found out the same night that the football player she was going to the coronation with had broken his collarbone so she didn't have a date either! So, Wendy saw an opportunity and took it and told Roman: "We might as well go together."

"Right," Roman said, smiling as Casey looked at them and frowned! Janay was pissed because she felt he shouldn't go if she wasn't going because they were supposed to be a couple! Yeah right! Roman told her he spent his money on a tuxedo and he was going to wear it! "I spent money for a dress!" she said pissed off which brings us to this argument now!

"Don't get mad at me because you didn't listen, get mad at yourself!" he told her, paying no attention to her tantrum! Click! She hung. He laughed.

~

Roman sat in his room on his bed and thought about the past few weeks. He thought about the fun he and Wendy had at the coronation and how well they clicked and he smiled as he thought about her smile or when she blushed and her dimples showed. They laughed, talked and enjoyed each other's company from the week of practice, the night of the coronation and afterwards and she was cool. He also thought about Janay and how she was more trouble than she was worth, but it was partially his fault! A week after the coronation they made up and had sex and the sex was good but not the place because he sexed the girl in his mom's bed and she and Frank came home early! He tried to cover his tracks, but Janay dropped a piece of jewelry in his mom's bed! He went into the bathroom trying to get her out the window when Faye started twisting the doorknob and beating on the bathroom door demanding that he open it! He tried to tell her he was using the bathroom, but she wasn't trying to hear it and when he opened the door she said, "Where is she?"

"Who?" Roman said, trying to feign ignorance and shake her, but the damage was done! She pulled the shower curtain back and there Janay stood trembling with some of her clothes still in her hands! Faye grabbed her and led her to the living room where she told her, "Little girl, if you were just a little older, I'd-" but she stopped herself and went to open the front door and told her to get out of her house then she turned her fury on Roman! *Whap!* the slap to his face sounded off and caught him off guard and "Mom!" was all he could say as he held his face.

"How could you?" she said furious and when he tried to say something else *Whap!* she slapped him again and told him, "You better get that girl home too!" and told him to get out! Roman did what Faye told him and got Janay home and when he came back, they were waiting for him. Frank was disappointed but understood a young boy trying to be a young man, but Faye was pissed off! She washed her sheets and put some more on their bed, then they had a long discussion, and Roman apologized over and over because he was wrong, dead wrong, but the flip side of it was Janay's attitude because, when he got to school, the next day, she tried to play him like he didn't exist and he laughed. She obviously didn't know who she was dealing with because his motto was: "I don't chase broads: broads chase me," so he left her alone and set his sights on this chick named Samantha, who he wanted to get with anyway because dudes thought she was untouchable. After all, no one at Carroll High had hit, *so who better than me* Roman said as he thought about how fine this chick was too! She was 5 9', jet black hair, dark eyes, a small waist, a pretty face, and a banging body! She was also captain of The Carrollettes which is the drill team at Carroll High School. Roman started paying attention to her and making conversation with her and she was reluctant at first because of his reputation and she didn't know if he was serious because he was the first guy who had enough confidence to step to her at her school but she liked that and she also found him funny and liked talking to him. He won her and Janay was hatin' but she played her hand and he played his and came up with Aces.

One day in gym class, which Samantha, Janay, him, and Ranay took together, Janay tried to test the waters because people were talking and she heard it. She didn't like it, but Roman had moved on, and it pained her that he did the breaking up and not her, and to flaunt it in front of her and everybody else was unacceptable in her sight!

"Roman! Roman come here!" she demanded to try to save face and turn this around as Roman walked by her and her twin! Samantha looked on with some of her friends as he stopped and turned around but she didn't have to worry because he was done with Janay and he just needed to make it clear.

"What's happening?" he asked coolly with other things on his mind.

Janay asked, "What is wrong with you and why haven't you called me?" trying to play this her way.

He sighed, then said, "Listen, we both know what happened, but I'm not tripping, and I don't know who you think you are but obviously you don't know who I am. One gone, put another one on."

Janay was pissed! "So that's it?" she said, waiting for his answer. "What do you think?" he said smartly and when he went to turn away, she slapped him and Ranay ran over to help her and everyone in the gym was shocked because before Roman knew what happened, he had slapped them both and watched them fall to the ground. Samantha ran and grabbed him as Roman was shaking his head and tripping off of what he had done while people held the twins back they cursed him out and tried to get to him again, Roman knew he had tripped out and he also knew he would be expelled and that's exactly what happened. He couldn't believe it, but his reaction was so fast. Now, he had to get back in school and he did; after going to the superintendent and getting that corporal punishment, he was reinstated and when he came back to school, the word was out that the twins were trying to get dudes to jump him, but he wasn't worried about that though because he could stand with his hands and anybody who knew him knew that too.

Roman and Samantha had been kicking it for a minute and the sex was off the chain! The first time they ditched school together, she put him right to sleep and all he could do was laugh. Faye liked her but knew her son never stayed in the same place for too long. He and Samantha went to movies together, games, dinner, family gatherings, and were considered the cutest couple on campus. He even escorted her to her debutante ball, otherwise known as her cotillion. When it was all said and done, she went back to an ex-boyfriend of hers who was an older guy. Roman wasn't tripping and, he respected her because she was honest about it and didn't play any games but took responsibility for her actions and the situation. Roman went back to doing what he knew how to do best: "play the field," which made his last year in school go faster. He still spent time with Jennifer when he could because she was working and attending Northeast University. He was hooking up with Angela Davis, who was attending Saint Frederick's High School and she was a straight sex kitten. He was also kicking it with Tanya, a chick from his old neighborhood on Burg Jones Lane who was attending Wossman High School. He was hittin' this chick from Neville High School named Ashanti who looked like a black Barbie doll and she was beautiful. He was also hittin' a chick named Sylvia who was No Holds Barred, meaning whatever and whenever! He was even knocking down this chick from West Monroe High School named Mona and was kicking it with four chicks from Ouachita High School and one, in particular, was his prom date. She was a bad chick who had a history with Janay and Ranay because Sonia was a twin with a sister named Tonia and both of them were beautiful and actually did a few modeling gigs. He was also hittin' a few chicks at Carroll and some in his neighborhood and nobody knew but him and them. Roman was thinking about all of this because of the decision he had just made. He was about to graduate and knew what he wanted to do after his graduation. He picked up the phone and made a call and they picked up on the fourth ring.

"Hello," they answered.

"What's up Dad?" he said ready to tell his father what he had decided to do.

"Nothing much, son. What about you?" Paul said, glad to hear from his son.

"I'm good, but guess what," Roman said.

"What?" Paul asked, curious now because of his tone.

"I joined the Army!" Roman told him.